Blazed

Breakers Hockey #8

Elise Faber

———

Hate missing Elise's new releases? Love contests, exclusive excerpts and giveaways?
Then signup for Elise's newsletter here!
www.elisefaber.com/newsletter

———

If you enjoy my series, considering supporting me on PATREON! Get access to early releases, bonus content, character art, audiobooks, and much more!
CLICK HERE TO SUPPORT ME>

———

And join Elise's fan group, the Fabinators (https://www.facebook.com/groups/fabinators) for insider information, sneak peaks at new releases, and fun freebies! Hope to see you there!

———

Breakers Hockey Series

<u>Breathless</u>

<u>Ballsy</u>

<u>Bewitched</u>

Blowout

Breathe

A Breakers Christmas

Blazed

Bound

Sierra Hockey Series

Over the Line

Caught from Behind

On the Fly

The Big Skate

Rush Hockey Trilogy #1

Big Puck Energy

Filthy Puckboy

So Pucking Over It

Rush Hockey Trilogy #2

Love, Pucks, and Other Stories

All's Fair in Pucks and War

No Pucks Lost Between Us

Rush Hockey Trilogy #3

Puck and Make Up

Blinded By Pucks

Match Made in Pucks

Eagles Hockey Series (all stand alone)

Broken Laces

Knotted Laces

Lace 'em Up

Billionaire's Club **(all stand alone)**

Bad Night Stand

Bad Breakup

Bad Husband

Bad Hookup

Bad Divorce

Bad Fiancé

Bad Boyfriend

Bad Blind Date

Bad Wedding

Bad Engagement

Bad Bridesmaid

Bad Swipe

Bad Girlfriend

Bad Best Friend

Bad Rebound

Bad Romance

Bad Business

Bad Billionaire's Quickies

Love, Action, Camera (all stand alone)

Dotted Line

Action Shot

Close-Up

End Scene

Meet Cute

***Love After Midnight* (all stand alone)**

Rum And Notes

Virgin Daiquiri

On The Rocks

Sex On The Seats

Life Sucks Series

Train Wreck

Hot Mess

Dumpster Fire

Clusterf*@k

FUBAR

Perfect Storm

Free Fall

Lost Cause

***Roosevelt Ranch Series* (all stand alone, series complete)**

Disaster at Roosevelt Ranch

Heartbreak at Roosevelt Ranch

Collision at Roosevelt Ranch

Regret at Roosevelt Ranch

Desire at Roosevelt Ranch

***Phoenix Series* (read in order)**

Phoenix Rising

Dark Phoenix

Phoenix Freed

Phoenix: LexTal Chronicles (rereleasing soon, stand alone, Phoenix world)

From Ashes

In Flames

To Smoke

KTS Series (all stand alone, series complete)

Riding The Edge

Crossing The Line

Leveling The Field

Scorching The Earth

Cocky Heroes World

Tattooed Troublemaker

About the Author

USA Today bestselling author, Elise Faber, loves chocolate, Star Wars, Harry Potter, and hockey (the order depending on the day and how well her team -- the Sharks! -- are playing). She and her husband also play as much hockey as they can squeeze into their schedules, so much so that their typical date night is spent on the ice. Elise is the mom to two exuberant boys and lives in Northern California. Connect with her in her Facebook group, the Fabinators or find more information about her books at www.elise-faber.com.

facebook.com/elisefaberauthor

amazon.com/author/elisefaber

bookbub.com/profile/elise-faber

instagram.com/elisefaber

tiktok.com/@elisefaberauthor

goodreads.com/elisefaber

Breakers Hockey Series

ONE

I gently squeeze the piping bag as I spin the turntable on which the perfectly frosted cake sits.

It sends a thin thread of icing out of the metal decorating tip, and I lean in, draping it carefully along the top edge of the confection.

Putting the finishing touches on the wedding cake that is the biggest I've ever made.

Six tiers.

Each coated in fluffy white buttercream smoothed to perfection.

And then further decorated, each tier with a different elegant white-on-white royal icing pattern that has my hands aching.

And my neck.

And my shoulders.

And my legs and ankles and feet.

Because—one more squeeze and I carefully pull away, set the piping bag on the metal table—I've been at this since three in the morning.

It's noon now.

And though I've been taking care of the rest of my duties that come with opening the bakery—namely baking the items that fill the cases so people can buy them and eat them and the business makes enough money so that I have a job (and, recently, a financial stake in the profits)—the rest of the time has been spent decorating the cake.

Busy.

Always.

The job. The bakery itself. My life.

Always busy.

Now I have less than an hour to box up the cake, stow it safely in the walk-in, and get my butt over to class.

I love decorating cakes.

It's a steady job that pays decently for a college student. It's a future, stable career—or that's what I tell myself, anyway.

But it isn't my dream.

It isn't—

"Did you leave any icing *on* the cake?"

I've just finished boxing said cake—or the top tier of said giant ass wedding cake, rather. Which is lucky. Because the man's voice has me jerking, my hand bumping into the cardboard.

And if the man—who, unfortunately, I recognize just from that single silken question, whose voice I know (and maybe still hear in my dreams)—had made me ruin this cake—or even just one layer of it—I might very well commit hockeycide.

As in, murder of the sexy, annoying hockey player currently leaning against the doorway that leads out into the front part of the bakery.

Walker Laine.

Who is standing there looking sexy with a big, strong body, tattoos, and a beard. He's wearing his typical uniform of a T-shirt and jeans that are encasing his thick thighs in a way that should be illegal.

Cupping them lovingly.

Reminding me how strong they are.

Pinning me onto the mattress. Holding me up as he fucks me against the wall.

Skating like wind on the ice.

My thighs tremble and I clench my teeth together sharply enough to send pain pulsing through my jaw. But, luckily, that jolt recenters me, and I manage to push down the hurt.

To settle on anger.

Something that's made easier when I notice that his annoying, kissable lips are turned up at the edges into a smirk.

And he has his arms crossed.

And his freaking ankles too as he reclines back against the open door.

Looking totally comfortable in my space. Invading my space.

Again.

For a man who supposedly doesn't like making connections with women, he seems to be doing that a lot. Crowding me in the waiting room of the hospital when my mom had a health scare and I was too upset to know what I was doing, too worried and anxious to keep him at arm's length. Driving me home after my mom turned the corner. Appearing at my mom's house to provide backup for the vitriol she likes to lob my way. Showing up at my place to check on me when those sharp, barbed words stung deeper than they should, considering that she's a bitter old woman and I've come to terms with the fact that she's never going to be the person I need. Coming to Christmas Eve dinner, invading my family time, sitting next to me, his thigh brushing mine, his arm pressing close, his scent in my nose. And now at...

My place of work.

A-*fucking*-gain.

So, yeah, rage makes the hurt disappear, and I narrow my eyes at him, pick up the boxed cake, and carry it to the walk-in refrigerator, stowing it on the shelf with the rest of the tiers. Tomorrow I'll stay late to finish everything up before going with Roy, our delivery guy, to the venue to set up the cake.

After which, I'll live with my hands in buckets of ice for twenty-four hours.

Sighing, I stand inside the walk-in and wipe my aching hands on my apron, which—as a certain annoying hockey player had pointed out—is covered in a small amount of icing.

Okay, a *lot* of icing.

Probably it's a comment on me that I work so messily. God knows, my mom says so. *Messy life, messy mind.* Which is fucking hilarious. Because my mom is a fucking disaster and just...

Not a good person.

That's why I ignore her shit and embrace my messiness—or try to, anyway.

Because it's not always that simple.

Parents—*mothers*—have the ability to wound deeply without even trying.

So, my apartment is clean. My car is immaculate. My aprons are...trashed. That's me.

And, more importantly, my cakes are perfect, even *if* I wear a piping bag's worth of icing each and every time I finish decorating—

"Ack!"

I ran into a brick wall.

No. Okay, fine. I ran into a brick-*headed* hockey player.

"What the fuck, Walker?" I snap, brushing off his hands, which come up to steady me—ugh, why does he have to be *nice?* —and start to move by him.

Even though he's smaller than a lot of the guys on the Breakers, Walker still takes up a lot of space. Or maybe that's only in my head. It's just...he seems big, too big, and he sucks all the air out of the room, and...he made me feel—

It doesn't matter.

What I felt that night *doesn't* matter.

Not when it comes to one Walker Laine.

"I need to talk to you," he says, snagging my arm, halting my escape.

"I think we've done all the *talking* we need to do," I snap, yanking free.

Regret careens across his face, marring the beautiful features.

Because once I thought that his invading my life meant something, that he might want something special with me.

Not just a place to stick his dick or free cookies or a woman to clean up his shit.

I thought he might want...*me*.

Just Dommie.

Just a girl who's no one special being wanted by a man who—

Made it abundantly clear a future that included wanting me wasn't in the cards for him.

"Sunlight—"

Yeah, no.

Calling me that, *now*, after what he said and how he pushed me away and...all he made me feel?

I can deal with the invading of my life, the annoying presence when I'm capable of handling my own shit. I can even deal with him showing up at my place. He wants to fix my sink? Sure, knock himself out.

But calling me Sunlight?

That can't happen.

And certainly not in that gentle voice paired with his hand lifting, fingers trailing down my throat.

That was what had given me the stupid hope, the thoughts of a future that might be.

That was what had hurt so fucking much when reality had smacked me back into my place.

"Don't," I snap.

His eyes flare with annoyance. "Dommie—"

I don't focus on that. I can't. Not when my gaze slides over his shoulder and I see the door to the walk-in slowly swinging shut.

Shit.

I lurch for it, but I'm too late.

It closes with a soft *click*.

One that can't even begin to demonstrate how fucked I am.

Because the door to the walk-in is broken. Because the freaking handle that's supposed to function to let someone out if the door shut on them doesn't actually work.

Because now I'm trapped in this goddamned giant refrigerator with Walker Laine.

"Shit!" I hiss, moving over to the handle and jabbing at it anyway.

No surprise, the door doesn't move.

"What's wrong?" he asks.

I glare over my shoulder at him, hoping he can see my fury in the dim overhead lights. "We're trapped," I growl. "The handle is broken, so we can't get out."

He's standing beneath one of those bulbs and I watch his brows drag together. "That seems dangerous. What if you're stuck in here and nobody is working?"

I let my glare intensify. "Well, I'm not *normally* confronted by annoying hockey players in the walk-in."

A beat as he appears unfazed by my laser eyes. "That didn't really answer my question, baby."

Baby. Ugh. Why does that send a flutter through my insides?

I turn back, wrestle with the handle again. "I'm always just in and out," but I'm unable to keep my gaze from his.

And those brows flick up, seeming to say, "That didn't really answer my question either."

I huff out a sigh. "*Normally,* I just call one of the other employees for help and they would come and let me out."

"So why don't you do that?"

Silence.

Annoying, long silence before I have to admit, "I don't have my phone."

His mouth quirks.

I hate him.

Detest him.

And I still think his little smirk is the sexiest thing I've ever seen.

"I have my phone," he says, pulling it out of his pocket and holding it up.

Thank God because—if I'm being truthful—I'm not sure I can yell loudly enough for them to hear me out front.

"But..." He tucks it away again, his voice transforming into velvet.

"What?" I ask, dread gathering in my belly.

That smirk widens.

"I'll only let you use it if you agree to go on a date with me."

Two

Dᴏᴍᴍɪᴇ

"You've made it clear that you don't date," I say, proud that my voice is even, that it doesn't betray the emotions in my belly, the feelings that are raking along the insides of my heart.

He shrugs.

Shrugs!

But it's his words that are the actual mindfuck.

"I was wrong."

He was *wrong*?

Is he actually serious right now?

"Look," I say, rubbing my forehead, at the throb blooming right above my left eyebrow, "just give me the phone and I'll call someone to let us out."

"Italian?" he asks, typing away at the screen of his cell. "I know a place that makes handmade pasta every day. You love a *cacio e pepe*, right? I've heard theirs is off the chart."

More typing.

But I barely register it because...*cacio e pepe.*

How the fuck does he know that?

"And they have a cannoli that's delicious"—his deep brown eyes lift from the screen of his cell, hit mine—"not as delicious as yours though, Sunlight."

"Don't," I hiss.

His gaze drops back down onto the screen. "You have class until five today, right?"

Another blip in my belly.

Because normally I go till three. Except once a month when I go to office hours and get out at—

"So," he goes on, "I'll swing by your apartment at five thirty."

—five.

I exhale shakily.

"We can eat early and get you home with plenty of time to do your homework and still have a full night's sleep before you have to be back here."

My heart is pounding a million miles per hour.

But...I hold on to the anger, lift my chin, and say, "You've lost your fucking mind."

He ignores me—and my anger—and taps a few more times. "There," he says. "Reservation made."

My mouth drops open. Then closes. "I'm not going to dinner with you," I grit out.

He leans against the metal wall and makes a deliberate show of tucking his phone away. "Then I guess we're both staying here for the foreseeable future."

I glare at him.

He grins. "Good thing I'm used to the cold."

This man is un-fucking-believable.

But I've made it my life mission—as of two seconds ago—to not give into assholes.

So instead of engaging further, I turn back to the door, willing my MacGyver skills to full strength. I can fashion a screwdriver out of one of the cake skewers and a piece of one of the shelves.

Totally.

Or I'll just use my Hulk strength to rip it to pieces.

No problem.

I stifle a groan, resist the urge to drop my head against the walk-in's metal door then to lift it again, then drop it again...and do it over and over until I'm in blissful unconsciousness.

"Bashing your head is going to hurt."

I freeze even though I *know* I didn't say that out loud.

Because...what the actual fuck?

I have MacGyver and Hulk skills and he's...Dr. Strange?

And clearly, I've spent too many hours left to my own devices in the back of this fucking bakery because I've gone delusional.

I sigh and drop my head forward, not gently either.

But before it can make contact with the metal panel, a palm hits my shoulder, drawing me back, another sliding around to the front of my face, cupping my forehead.

Stopping me before my forehead *thunks* against the door.

"Don't," he murmurs. "Don't do that, baby."

My heart thuds and I try to stop my body from melting against him, *really* I do.

But even though I lock my knees and tense my abs, I still do the same dumbass shit.

I melt.

Against him.

His hands move, arms shifting, wrapping around me, wrapping me in a big, warm, strong hockey player.

His scent fills my nose, reminding me of that night. When he filled me to the brim. When he rocked my world. When he made me think that—

"Let go," I whisper.

"Don't hurt yourself," he orders.

"Because that's *your* job?" I ask.

His body tenses around me, hands tightening, muscles in his arms standing out sharply in relief. "That was below the belt, Sunlight."

"Let me go," I counter, even as a tiny blip of guilt winds through my belly. *He* hurt me. *He* pushed me away. *He* deserves it.

A sigh that ruffles through my hair. "Go to dinner with me."

"I don't negotiate with terrorists."

His sigh turns into a chuckle. "You know I'll show up anyway."

I do know this.

Unfortunately.

"Give me your phone," I order.

He spins me in the circle of his arms, chocolate eyes on mine. "Five thirty, baby?"

Baby.

Fuck. Why does that make me shiver?

His eyes warm, going full-on melted chocolate. "Yeah," he murmurs. "Five-thirty."

I open my mouth to snap at him, but he's moving, reaching into his pocket, pulling out his cell and setting it into my palm.

Fine.

The man can be delusional and think I've just agreed to going on his stupid date.

I'll just...be mysteriously absent from my apartment at five thirty.

Only...why do I have the sinking sensation that this man will track me down?

Before I can worry about that, though, I'm glancing down at the phone in my palm, hitting the button on the side and preparing to ask him to unlock the screen.

Only it doesn't light up.

I press the button again.

Still black.

This man is messing with me.

I hold the button down on the side, wait to see the logo pop up on the screen.

Only nothing happens.

Okay, well, *something* does.

But it's not what I *want* to happen.

A battery symbol appears, empty except for a narrow strip of red at the bottom.

What. The. *Actual*. Fuck?

"What's the delay, Sunlight?" he asks, mouth twitching. "Unless you want to have our date in this fridge? I'm cool with it" —he smirks—"you can just cuddle up to me when you get cold."

There's a little cord symbol on the screen.

Telling me to. Plug. It. In.

Because the fucking battery is dead.

D.E.A.D.

Dead.

Like this goddamned sexy hockey player in front of me is about to be.

Three

Walker

She turns to me and for a second, I have the urge to step back.

Out of arm's reach.

Then I remember myself.

Remember who I am.

Remember that I outweigh this tiny woman by at least a hundred pounds, and have a good six inches on her.

I can crush her like a bug.

Any time I touch her, I have to pay attention to my strength, have to make sure I don't hurt her.

Because it would be too easy.

Only I *had* hurt her.

Just not physically.

Guilt razors through me.

I have my reasons for handling Dommie the way I had—not that I'm trying to justify them or discount that I *had* hurt her or that she felt that way in the first place. I just...

Have my reasons.

She lifts her hands like she's going to shove me then stops, clenches them into fists at her sides, my cell clutched in one so tightly I swear that I hear it creak in protest.

"Are you fucking serious right now?" she yells.

My brows drag together because...that's escalated quickly. "What are you talking about, baby?"

Now her hand comes up so fast that I rock back.

But she's not trying to hurt me.

She's...showing me my phone. Something I've seen before. *Okaaay.*

I shrug. "Just make the call, Sunlight."

Her coffee-colored eyes narrow. "I would love to"—she makes air quotes—"*make the call*. But I freaking can't."

"Oh," I say, reaching for the cell, realizing that the screen's locked and she won't know my passcode.

When it doesn't automatically light up, when I slip it from her hand, I press the button on the side.

Nothing happens.

What—?

I press the button again, then again, and once more for good measure, like I somehow forgot how to push things and need to hone my skills by practicing on repeat. Or maybe it's more like if I keep doing it that's going to somehow change the outcome.

But, newsflash, nothing changes.

I jab at the button, this time holding it down, waiting for my cell to boot up.

Something finally happens.

Just not what I *want* to happen.

"It's dead," I mutter.

"Yeah, genius," she snaps. "It's fucking dead."

I look around the inside of the walk-in, as though I can summon up a charger and an outlet. But it's just shelf after shelf of confection—some in white cardboard boxes, but most sitting in huge metal trays, their rainbow of colors on display.

Something this bakery was known for.

Delicious beauty.

Theo told me that Dommie came up with the branding when she signed on as a partner in the bakery and the owner, Ren, let her take the lead in the refresh. Just like she came up with the logo that's now stamped onto those white cardboard boxes. Rebranding. Changing recipes. Social media strategy. She worked her ass off to improve the business, and it's turning record profits, so much so that Ren has been able to step back for the first time in decades.

And Dommie's done it mostly by working hard, but also by leaning into the *beauty* of the desserts, decorating even the simplest cupcake with intricate touches that make them tiny works of art that are documented on social media.

And then are eaten.

Those beautiful desserts have become staples of this shop.

And the reason she's become a partner.

No surprise, because—despite the example set by their mother—the Moreno siblings all work their asses off in their separate pursuits.

They don't shy away from difficult tasks or long hours or hustling to get ahead.

Considering that's how I managed *my* current pursuit, I respect that energy.

But she's also a full-time college student, and she helps take care of her mother (because even though the Moreno matriarch is not a family favorite, her children aren't shoving her into a home like I would have).

Doctor's appointments.

Food in her fridge.

Looking after their younger brother—something made easier now that Jer has graduated high school and is taking a gap year to travel the world.

And running a business and getting straight As—because, of course, she is.

And...being locked in a walk-in refrigerator without a jacket and goose bumps prickling on her skin and...

A dead phone.

I look from the screen to her eyes, the gold flakes in them reminiscent of sunlight glinting off glass, blinding me with their beauty.

Blinding me with her *rage*.

But then her lids slide closed and she drops her chin to her chest, exhaling deeply.

Banking that anger.

Tucking away her emotions.

I saw her sister do that a lot before she and Theo got together, before she had someone to take her back when shit got real.

Eva doesn't do that shit anymore—mostly because Theo won't let her.

I'm not about to let Dommie continue on that same toxic path.

Definitely not now, when things have...

Changed.

I'll leave it at that.

I couldn't pursue Dommie a few months ago, not really—because *reasons*—but shit is different now, and I'm done with watching her kill herself.

"Don't," I order softly.

She frowns.

"Don't hide yourself from me."

That frown deepens.

"You're pissed," I say. "That's fine. You're allowed to be pissed at me. I came into your space and got you locked in a giant refrigerator."

Her eyes narrow. "So, once we get out of here, you're going to leave me alone?"

"Fuck no," I tell her. "We have dinner reservations."

Golden sparks flashing, turning into molten sunshine.

Fury.

Sexy as fuck.

Is it weird that I want her to yell at me some more? That I

want her to yell at me until I lose patience and kiss the sass right out of her?

Probably.

But as she shivers, arms crossing over her chest, I remember that I have bigger problems.

A fridge handle that doesn't work.

An empty kitchen beyond.

A cell phone with a dead battery.

And a woman I want to be mine...

Who's cold.

Four

We have dinner reservations.

Fucking *dinner* reservations.

This asshole has us trapped and his phone is dead and it's getting cold in here, especially when I'm not moving, when I'm not hefting big ass bags of flour and huge mixing bowls and trays laden with desserts, when I'm not tensing every single muscle in my body, holding perfectly still except for my hands, trying to get the perfect drape of royal icing.

I shiver, rub my hands along the outsides of my bare arms.

Short sleeves and walk-ins aren't the greatest.

Neither are annoying hockey players and empty kitchens.

Or—

"Come here."

I blink, not processing the words before he's wrapping his arms around me, bringing his big, strong—*warm*—body against mine.

"What—"

But his hand is already on the back of my head, pressing my face to his throat.

He immediately hisses and I tense, but he doesn't release me as he rumbles, "Your nose is cold."

"Yeah," I grumble, even though my heart is launching itself against my rib cage, even though my pulse is pounding in my veins, the thrumming noise so damned loud in my ears that I can barely hear myself continuing talking, throwing out sass because it's the only way to survive an Attack by Sexy Hockey Player. "That's what happens when someone locks me in a refrigerator in only a T-shirt."

"And a filthy apron that's probably getting my clothes filthy."

"You deserve it," I grit out.

"Damn right, I do." A rough chuckle, his hand smoothing up and down my back, using friction to warm me, even though the moment his body had engulfed mine, the cold couldn't begin to bother me, anyway (hello, Elsa, I see you walking into the party like you own the damn thing).

Losing it, Dommie,

Yup.

"But I won't take *all* the credit for the locking," he says. "It's not like I ripped the handle off to keep you locked up, evil genius style."

"I wouldn't put that past you," I mutter.

Another chuckle, this one taking on the slightest bit of silk. "If I'd known locking you in here was the fastest way to get you into my arms again, I would have done it weeks ago."

I narrow my eyes, but I can't glare at him, not like I want to, not with him still holding me close, one hand still gently rubbing my back, the other sliding into my hair, dislodging my bun, weaving into the tendrils at my nape and keeping my face in his throat.

The spicy scent of him.

The stubble of his beard catching in my hair.

The broad, warm strength.

The hold that is firm and confident.

All of it is...nice.

Okay, fine, it's *more* than nice. It's fucking intoxicating. It brings all the memories, the sensations, the yearning to the forefront of my mind.

And I barely survived it the first time around.

And that was...barely anything at all.

No. It was *nothing* at all.

"So," he says, apparently not in any hurry to let me go even though I've gone stiff, the memories, the embarrassment eating at my insides, "how long until someone realizes the kitchen is empty?"

I pause, considering that.

It's midmorning, and I've only got one staffer out front.

Another is supposed to come in to help with the afternoon rush because when the middle school—located just a couple of blocks over—lets out, the kids beeline here to load up on goodies.

Great for the bottom line.

Not so good for the chaos they sometimes create.

Eleven to fourteen-year-olds are not for the faint of heart.

So, how long until Sonya notices I didn't come out to say goodbye before leaving for my classes?

Will she notice?

Or will Tom when he comes in?

Or will neither of them realize that my stuff is still in the kitchen and my car in the lot but that I'm missing?

I sigh.

The last one. I know it.

They won't realize that we're locked in here until they come to restock the cases in preparation for the middle schoolers' hollow legs.

"Fuck," I mutter, dropping my head more heavily against Walker's shoulder.

Stupid.

But also...*fuck.*

"The answer is that good?" he asks softly.

I just groan in response.

Silence, but those hands are still moving—one through my hair, one at my back. Then his voice goes light. "At least we won't starve?"

I groan again, finally finding the strength to lift my head from all of that warmth, to slip away from the firm, confident hold. He lets me go this time, allows me to step out of his embrace, but he doesn't really step away, so even though I put some distance between us, he's still right there.

Right *freaking* there.

Gorgeous even in the dim lights of the fridge, the shadows highlighting the strong lines of his nose, his jaw, the fading scar on his cheek.

I had gently kissed that scar, not long after the stitches had come out, the line red and angry instead of the pale pink it was now.

I look away, shove down the urge to kiss it again.

To soothe the old hurt.

This man is the one who cuts—he doesn't need soothing.

Which is why I don't launch myself back into his arms when the cool air begins to creep in.

It's why I allow my back to find the cold steel of the fridge door, why I allow my knees to buckle as I sink down onto the floor.

Why I curl up into a ball and bury my face in my arms.

And pretend this isn't happening.

Because that's all I have the strength to do.

Hide. Pretend it doesn't hurt.

And move on.

A freaking Moreno Special.

Five

Walker

I stare down at the woman who's gone full protective ball, and I want to put my fist through the metal panels lining the inside of the fridge.

I don't because I would certainly hurt myself and I need these fucking hands to keep working so I can do my damned job.

I don't because it'll probably scare her and I don't want to do that.

I don't because...I deserve to be hurting, deserve to take this hit.

I did this.

Rubbing a hand over my face, I sink down next to her, ignoring that her shoulders hitch up, nearly covering her ears, clearly not loving that I'm crowding her.

But...

We're here.

I have one shot at this and—

"I'm sorry," I say.

Those shoulders hitch higher, the fist that I can see tightening until her knuckles stand out in sharp relief.

Fuck.

"I...had my reasons to handle things how I did," I say, ignoring her fist clenching even more.

Silence.

Long enough that my nape starts to go all prickly, that I open my mouth to keep talking when she finally replies.

"You had your *reasons,*" she says, so quietly that I almost miss the deadly edge to her tone.

Almost.

"Yeah," I tell her. "I had reasons, and no, they weren't good enough. No they won't justify how much of an ass I was, but I can't go back. I can't make it so it didn't happen. It did. I was a dick and I hurt you." I hold her eyes when she finally lifts her head and looks at me. "And I'm sorry."

Coffee-colored irises holding mine.

Then she exhales, lids closing, chin dropping back to her folded arms. "I know you are," she says so quietly that I barely hear it, so quietly that I strain to make out the words. "It's fine."

"It's not."

Her head comes up again, gaze hitting mine. "It's fine," she says again.

"It's not," *I* say again.

Nostrils flaring as she inhales. "I told you, I'm fine."

"*You* may be fine, but what I did wasn't."

Her lips press flat, release. "Because of your *reasons.*"

I nod.

"*Reasons* you aren't going to divulge."

It takes everything in me to not shudder. The thought of anyone knowing the shit that was going on in my life at that time makes me want to punch something.

Either that or blow chunks.

"Reasons I'm not going to divulge," I tell her.

Her head tilts to the side, ponytail swinging behind her, expression not open exactly, but there's a dash of curiosity in the deep brown depths of her eyes.

I wait for her to ask—to demand—I give her an explanation. But...

It's Dommie.

She doesn't expect that much—not from men, not from people who've disappointed her, certainly not from me, a person who's both.

So, no, she doesn't ask, just leans back against the door, head *thunking* gently against the metal, throat exposed. I want to bend my head, press my nose to her throat, to inhale the scent of her, commit it to memory.

It's been so long since our nights together that I can't remember all the various notes of her smell. Flowers and vanilla, woman and sweet. Hints of tart and spice, belying the fire she had inside her.

And something delicate.

Something I could never place, even though I had gone full creep and studied her shampoo bottles and lotion and even Googled her perfume.

It was just...Dommie.

"Are you cold?" I blurt out.

Her eyes flick open and she arches a brow.

Right. It's cold in here and she's in a T-shirt.

I finally get my head out of my ass, start lifting up my shirt, which—and I'm enough of an asshole to get a bolt of pleasure from—has her eyes going wider, her mouth dropping open, her cheeks going bright pink—

"What are you doing?" she gasps.

The cold hits my stomach, my chest, but I don't feel it.

Not really.

Not with her gaze on the growing expanse of bared flesh.

Nope. I'm plenty warm, even with most of the blood in my body heading straight for my dick.

"You're cold," I say, pulling my shirt the rest of the way off, leaning forward, and tugging it over her head.

It dwarfs her, tiny woman that she is.

"Y-you—" Her eyes are wide as she sputters her way through the opening at the neckline. "You can't just take off your shirt!"

"It's not Superglued to me," I point out. "And you're cold."

"And now you're half-naked—" Those cheeks grow even more pink. "You can't be half-n-naked in here. W-with me!"

I shrug, lean back against the fridge door, gritting my teeth together when my skin hits the icy cold metal, pretending it's fine when it's fucking awful. But I'm not taking my shirt back—and not just because her stare is glued to my chest (if I can't gain a second chance with my winning personality, I'll take her being attracted to me to get one). It's also not because she looks fucking adorable swimming in the fabric of my shirt.

It's because she's cold.

And now I've done something to make that better.

Instead of adding to the bad and making shit worse.

"Walker!" she snaps, reaching for the hem of the shirt.

I catch her hand, draw it toward me, pressing it flat to my chest, ignoring the way my cock twitches—or maybe enjoying it. Either way, I hold fast when she tries to pull it away, and draw her nearer.

"Fucking stop it right now," she snaps. "You're being stupid. I'm fine and—"

I bend down so our faces are close, our lips are almost touching.

"What are you doing?" she whispers.

I wind my free hand into her hair, further dislodging the bun that she wears to work. I fucking hate it, hate how it hides the silken strands, how it hides that beauty of her. "Keeping you warm."

"I didn't ask for your T-shirt," she murmurs as I tilt her face up.

"I know."

"And I don't—"

But she doesn't get the rest of her sentence out because I lean in and close the distance between our mouths.

Six

Dommie

He's all around me.

Not just his shirt.

But his arms, his torso, his hands and lips and...

All of him.

And it's fucking great.

It takes me right back to my apartment, right back to my bed.

I should pull back. That would be the smart thing, the safe thing, but...I've missed this.

Too fucking much to tear my mouth from his.

Too much to not part my lips, to let him inside, to surrender to his kiss.

"*Fuck*," he growls, drawing me closer, drawing me onto his lap, coaxing my legs onto either side of him until I'm straddling his waist, sitting on the hard length of his cock, rocking against him, my pussy remembering exactly how good it felt to have him stretching me as he stroked deep, remembering exactly how he fucked me hard and fast and a little rough, all that strength of his in careful control.

Never taking it too far.

But riding the razor's edge in a way that had me experiencing the most intense orgasms of my life.

"That's it, baby," he rasps as he breaks his mouth away from mine, his hand dropping to my hip, grinding me harder against him. "Let me feel that pussy rub against me."

My hips are moving of their own volition. My body instinctively seeking the satisfaction it knows this man can provide.

I lean forward, dropping my hands against his bare chest, feeling the strong planes of muscles there. Then his mouth is on mine again and I'm...lost.

In his lips and teeth and tongue.

In his body and mine and how perfectly they move together.

In the soft rumbles of his groan as his tongue dances over mine, as his chest presses close, as his hands work their way under the layers of shirts and my apron and skate over my bare skin.

Up. Up. *Up*.

Slipping beneath the band of my bra, running roughened fingertips over the curves of my breasts, skating them in until—

"*Oh!*" I gasp, hips jerking.

"So fucking pretty," he mutters, rolling my nipples between his fingers, grinding up against me. "I've dreamed about these tits, Sunlight, dreamed about slipping into that pussy, feeling it tighten around me, dreamed about hearing—"

"Walker!" My head drops back as pleasure wells up within me, threatens to spill over.

"Dreamed about hearing you call my name as you come on my dick." His fingers tighten and I moan again, my orgasm *right* there. "Dreamed about falling asleep with you in my arms, just so I can wake you up in the middle of the night and fuck you all over again, just so I can watch and hear you come again."

Heat gathers at the base of my spine, and I'm lost.

There's absolutely no thought given to the fact that I'm dry humping a man I don't like (or a man I'm pretending *not* to like anyway because I'm hurt).

There's absolutely no regard given to me doing this dry

humping inside a fridge filled with confections I made, at my place of business, my livelihood. I own a piece of this company—more than a piece, actually.

I own half.

My future, as much as I'm not sure I want it.

My past, definitely.

And I'm grinding against a hard dick, forgetting about the cold, the consequences.

Forgetting about everything except my impending orgasm, the pleasure that awaits me, how this man feels when he kisses and touches and strokes me.

"Oh God!" I groan as I finally tip over the edge, plummeting into a pool of pleasure and oblivion and...

Walker.

The man who is everything I ever wanted...and everything I can't have.

Because he didn't want me, and made that explicitly clear.

And I'm not ever going to be with a man who doesn't value me.

His hands release my breasts and run along my flesh, arms wrapping around me, pulling me close, burying his face in my hair, inhaling deeply. "Fuck, baby," he murmurs roughly. "Fuck, you are so goddamned beautiful."

I want to believe that.

I want him to mean that.

But...

There's a groan, the screech of metal against metal, and—

Shit.

I sit back, rip off Walker's shirt, and thrust it at him, ignoring his grunt.

Probably because it's paired with me clambering off him, and not doing it gracefully.

Because I know what that screeching noise is.

It's the cart we use to reload the cases, and it's being rolled from the front of the store...heading for the fridge.

Heading for *us*.

"Put your fucking shirt on," I hiss.

He's already moving, tugging it over his head, yanking it down his body, covering all those glorious muscles in frosting-stained fabric. "What is it—?"

But then the fridge handle is turning, the big heavy door is swinging outward.

Warmth immediately swarms me, almost too hot now, embarrassment mingling with heat from the ovens and leftover blood pumping from my orgasm. Immediately, my palms go clammy and a bead of sweat drips down between my breasts.

My knees wobble, but I lock them, hold my ground.

Fingers wrap around my elbow.

A strong body comes close.

No, a *warm,* strong body comes close.

And it's too much—too much closeness, too much heat.

Too much Walker.

But then the door is swinging wider, revealing Sonya and Tom and the huge rolling cart they'll load with trays, saving trips back and forth to the case so they can restock.

Sonya gasps, her eyes going wide, her mouth dropping open. Tom isn't much better, letting go of the cart, sending it rolling backward.

"Um," Sonya says.

I force a smile, glance down at my watch. "Well," I squeak. *Christ.* I clear my throat, pretend this is just all in a day's work. "The handle was stuck again. Thanks for letting us out." Thankfully, my voice is even, absent now of even the slightest bit of embarrassment or shame.

Kudos to my mom for helping me bury those emotions so deeply that no one will ever be able to see them.

Unless I let them.

Which will happen...*fucking never.*

I breeze by them, yanking my apron over my head, shoving it

into the dirties bin on my way down the hall to the office. I tug open the bottom drawer, pull out my purse, then straighten.

And freeze.

Walker is standing in the doorway again, arms crossed over his chest, big body taking up way too much fucking space.

"Dinner," he says. "I'll see you at five thirty."

I open my mouth, preparing to tell him to fuck right off, but he's already moving, turning and giving me a flashing glimpse of his back before he starts sauntering down the hall, disappearing from sight.

Leaving me with those dangerous words.

And a throbbing clit.

SEVEN

Grunting, I let the weights drop back into the cradle, sitting there for a second because my muscles are protesting.

But there's no fucking around today.

I don't have time.

Need to get this shit done.

Then get showered.

Then head over to Dommie's early because I know she's going to do her best to avoid me.

Not going to happen.

Or, rather, I'm not going to *allow* it to happen.

So...getting my shit done, getting the fuck out, and then playing creeper at Dommie's place.

Cornering her so she can't escape.

Muahaha.

Right.

When I start channeling Evil Inner Genius, it's time to call it on the weights.

I snag my towel, wipe at my forehead, then make my way out

of the gym. The space was remodeled over the summer—a perk of winning the Cup twice in the last few years. But those wins mean the team now has a new locker room space (including tankless water heaters that several of my teammates are way too fucking in love with...long, hot showers for the win), a revamped gym, and a refurbished rec room/kitchen space.

There are gaming chairs and big-screen TVs.

A full kitchen for whoever the fuck wants to cook (even though we get shit catered and there's plenty of premade food available at all times).

A ping pong table—because we get competitive about so many things, but especially about ping pong.

And the aforementioned brand-new gym. Along with a cool plunge pool, a sauna, a hot tub, and a brand-new PT suite.

All the things we need to be successful, to stay healthy, to keep us at the top.

Aside from the roster, that is.

And the team coming together and the camaraderie in the locker room.

And the lines gelling at the right moment.

And the hockey gods smiling on us.

And fate. And luck.

And—

I freeze as I take in the rec room.

I was expecting it to be empty because a lot of the guys are still working out. Or, if anything, to find only a teammate or two grabbing something to drink or eat, maybe getting a head start on the latest NHL video game.

I definitely don't expect to find Jackson and Claire occupying the space.

Don't expect to see sunshiney, nothing-bothers-her Claire wearing a thunderous expression with Jackson hovering close, his face millimeters from hers.

Hmm.

Part of me is tempted to spy and report back to Smitty, our

resident gossip-trader. The rest of me knows I've got my own woman who often wears a thunderous expression...also only when it's directed toward me.

And I don't want Smitty sticking his nose in that just yet.

Just *yet*, because I know it's inevitable, and I've accepted it. I just...don't want it...*yet*.

Which is why I don't linger—and I sure as shit don't report this newest going-on.

Avoiding Smitty's crosshairs, but also because I really need to get the fuck out of here if I'm going to have a proper stakeout of Dommie's place.

I bypass the kitchen—and the fridge that Claire appears to be in the middle of restocking.

I bypass the recliners and the couch, avoid the lure of the gaming system.

I bypass the door to the sauna.

I run into trouble as I round the ping pong table.

Because the fuckers known as my teammates are like goddamned children who can't clean up after themselves.

I miss the ball on the floor—because while I might not be reporting this bit of gossip to Smitty, that doesn't mean I'm not soaking up every single detail of the tense moment between Claire and Jackson, a former prospect, but now an important part of the roster.

So, I'm being fucking nosy as shit, and karma decides to teach me a lesson.

Probably because I managed to lock a woman in a fridge earlier today.

Okay, it's probably because I hurt a woman who's as damn near close to perfect as they come.

Because...*reasons*.

God, I'm an asshole.

Which is probably another *probably* as to why that ball decided to enact its revenge.

I step.

I *slip*.

I nearly fall right on my fucking head, catching myself on the edge of the table, and making *all* the fucking noise I was trying to avoid.

After I've prevented death by ping pong ball, I glance over at the kitchen, see that, unfortunately, I've garnered the attention of the previously occupied couple.

No longer canoodling—or glaring from only a couple of millimeters away—they are staring at me.

Glaring at *me*.

"Don't mind me," I say cheerfully. "I was just leaving."

"Walker," Jackson begins, his tone bordering on deadly.

"I'm really *just leaving*," I say, holding his eyes, silently communicating that while I *am* leaving, most of the team is in the next room, so that if he wants to keep whatever the fuck is going on between him and our former intern—and current Gen Z social media guru—he needs to cool it and get his shit together.

He narrows his eyes, keeps glaring, but the twitch of his mouth tells me he's reading me loud and clear.

I flick my brows up, turn my glance at Claire, silently communicating the same thing.

She, smart woman that she is, gives a tiny nod then turns away from me, from Jackson, and gets the fuck out of the room.

The moment the door shuts behind her, he's in my face. "You breathe one word of this—"

"Look, man," I mutter. "I've got enough shit on my plate without alerting the Smitty Gossip train. But if *you* want to avoid that—" I tilt my head toward the gym. "Then you need to tighten up your shit, get your head out of your ass, and treat Claire like the fucking goddess she is."

A growl as he steps closer, the toes of his shoes brushing mine. "If you fucking touch her—"

"I don't want her."

I like Claire. She's a cool chick—smart, funny, gorgeous. But my focus is on another woman, one who's smarter, who's funnier, who's so fucking beautiful it takes my breath away. But, at the same time, Claire is one of us, has been with the team for long enough that she is like a little sister.

And I don't want any assholes fucking with her.

Not even an asshole I consider my friend.

Jackson narrows his eyes.

"You asshole," I say, going full caveman. "Claire awesome."

Those stormy gray eyes narrow further.

"Don't fuck with her unless you're prepared to take it all the way."

I turn away before the glare can become something else—for example, a ping pong paddle up my ass—and move out into the hall, avoiding eye contact and any potential conversations.

No last-minute chats with Coach.

No stopping by the PT suite to talk about my touchy hamstring that's healing, but not as fast as I or the trainers want.

No getting waylaid by the other half of the social team and being stuck trading fucking friendship bracelets or some shit.

Nope. I avoid all of that and make it out into the parking garage, climb into my car.

Then I drive home, slogging my way through afternoon traffic.

And *then*, after a rapid-fire shower, I drive over to Dommie's.

And I begin my creepy stakeout.

EIGHT

DOMMIE

"And then, I'll expect to see drafts of your business plans by next Thursday," my professor says, closing out the slide deck and rounding the wide metal and wood desk that takes up most of the space in front of the whiteboard.

He leans against the corner, crossing his ankles, confident and comfortable, the movement pulling his pale blue button down taut across his chest.

I hear the girl next to me sigh and lean toward her friend, a thin blond who can't grow a mustache to save his soul, but who's trying to anyway. "What I wouldn't give to undo those buttons," she whispers.

Mustache smirks. "I think you might struggle with those nails"—a nod at the long, pink talons she's sporting—"clearly, I'm much better suited to the task." He holds up his own hand, nails meticulously groomed.

She pauses, head tilting, perfectly wavy curls bouncing as she considers that. "Okay, so you undo the buttons and we both worship that perfectly sculpted chest."

Considering our professor is still talking, telling us that his scheduled office hours have changed for the next week, I try to tune them out. Unfortunately, part of me is thinking that they don't have any clue as to what a perfectly sculpted chest looks like —because they haven't seen Walker's.

Luckily, the rest of my brain is listening to the new times and dates and figuring out how to make my schedule work if I need to actually attend any of them.

Because I have so many freaking cake orders.

And custom cookies to decorate.

And—

There's a sudden burst of noise—people gathering their bags and computers, notebooks and water bottles, battered wooden chairs groaning in protest, tiny desktops squealing angrily as they're shoved back to the side and tucked away.

I push all thoughts of baked goods away and focus on getting packed up, needing to get to my next class—

"Ms. Moreno," my professor says, staying me. "Wait just a moment."

Great. Now I feel like I've been called to the principal's office.

I look up from my backpack, having just shoved my laptop into the compartment and see my professor is coming toward me.

The pair who'd been crooning about his perfectly sculpted chest glare at me, hesitating in the row of desks as our professor ascends the last couple of steps and pauses in front of me.

He glances toward Mustache and Friend. "I'll see you both in class next week," he says. "And I'm looking forward to a *complete*" —there's a strong emphasis on complete—"assignment this time, Hayley."

The blonde colors, but nods quickly, ducking her head. "Of course, Professor Johnson."

"And Kurt," he says to Mustache, "you'll be at office hours on Monday? We need to go over your last exam."

Mustache—er, *Kurt*—nods, pink coating his cheeks. "Yes, Professor Johnson."

"Good." A nod. "Then I'll see you both next week."

This time it's a clear dismissal, and Hayley and Kurt both take it, grabbing their bags and moving up the stairs and out of the rapidly emptying classroom.

I turn back to my professor, bracing for the inevitable disappointment he's about to toss my way.

"Dominique—"

"Dommie," I correct instinctively because I hate my prissy birth name, and *dumbly* because that's not what's important when Professor Johnson is likely going to fail me.

"I know I've been slipping a bit on my assignments," I say—also dumbly because highlighting my shortcomings isn't a smart play in a business class. "I promise that my business plan will be really good—"

"Your assignments are the best in the class," he says without preamble, sending my pulse skittering. "But that's not why I wanted to speak with you."

"Oh." I pause, resisting the urge to nibble at my bottom lip.

"There's a faculty dinner tonight," he says.

I frown. Wait for an explanation that'll have the out-of-the-blue statement making sense.

Because I'm not faculty.

"It's tradition for us to all bring a student we think is excelling in our respective programs," he says. "We talk shop, brainstorm ideas for internships, and make connections with other students and teachers who align with your goals and resources..."

Whoa.

That sounds amazing.

Maybe *too* amazing—like it's going to come with strings attached and regret and—

"...so, if you're available tonight, it's being held at..." He names a restaurant off-campus but just around the corner. One of the typical haunts for students and faculty alike.

"I—" My mind flashes back to what I've been trying (and failing) to avoid thinking about...

Walker.

His perfectly sculpted chest and thighs and abs and dick.

His gorgeous face and eyes I can fall into. *Had* fallen into. Eyes that sold me a dream I can't have.

He'll be waiting at my apartment. I know he will be.

Pushing me.

Crowding me.

Wearing me down until we end up at that restaurant.

And part of me will enjoy it, will crave more, will be so fucking hurt again when I end up having it torn away from me again.

All of that flashes through my mind in a second, tears through me, claws raking my insides, and even though I'm about to decline—because something about the way Professor Johnson is staring at me, waiting for my answer, sends the hairs on my nape prickling—I open my mouth and ask, "What time is it happening?"

"Five thirty."

I freeze, nape no longer prickling, tossing up a thanks to the universe for giving me this out, and say, "Yes. I would love to come, Professor Johnson. Thank you."

He smiles, and even though this man doesn't do it for me in the least—thick hockey boys have ruined rangy, leanly muscled academics for me—I have to admit that that man has a nice smile. "Todd," he says, smile widening, reaching out and squeezing my shoulder. "Professor Johnson always makes me feel ancient."

More prickles, but before I can really listen to that instinct, Professor Johnson—*Todd*—is turning away, bounding down the stairs, saying over his shoulder, "See you later, Dominique."

"Dommie," I correct softly, but he's already too far away to hear, unplugging his laptop from the dongle, tucking it into his messenger bag, and I stand there for a second before I realize I'm staring, so I turn back to my backpack, shove the rest of my things in, engage the zippers.

I grab my coat, shrug it on, and then I'm calling out my

goodbye and heading for the door, having to hustle to make it to my next class on time.

The freezing ass blast of wind that hits me in the face has me moving quickly between buildings and inside, down the hall to my next classroom.

Sitting in an empty chair at one of the wide tables that make up this section's seating.

I pull out my things, get settled mere seconds before my professor starts speaking.

No time to think.

No time to process what I agreed to, what Walker would think.

Focus.

Work.

Avoid.

The motto of my life.

NINE

WALKER

I was early enough.

I know I was.

But she hasn't shown up.

Even though I've been sitting in my car, turning on the engine occasionally so I don't freeze my dick off.

I have eyes on her front door and on her parking spot, and she isn't here, hasn't been here.

Not unless she's pulling some fucking secret agent moves and crawling in through a two-story window or some shit.

But then again, I would see some lights on or a flashlight beam or something.

So, why is the *Mission Impossible* theme song playing through my mind?

Probably because my dumbass has been sitting here for hours —and hours past five thirty—freezing.

I sigh, turn on the engine for the last time, and reach down to shift into reverse, intending to back out, to retreat from this battle —albeit not the war—but the moment my hand touches the gearshift, I'm blocked in by a car that pulls into the parking lot.

"Christ," I mutter, sighing as I drop my palm away, waiting—now impatiently because I've reached my limit and I'm ready to get the fuck all out of there.

But that impatience fades a heartbeat later when the car continues driving forward...and pulls into Dommie's spot.

But it's not Dommie's car.

Frowning, I watch the driver's door open and a man round the hood, going to the passenger's side.

Probably someone dropping off a date.

It's a dick move to use Dommie's spot, but—

"What the fuck?" I turn off my car, grab the handle, and shove open my door as *Dommie* gets out of the passenger's side.

She teeters.

The man catches her arm and I can see by her body language that she doesn't like that.

I'm already moving across the lot as she pulls away from the man, the wind blasting, sending slices of icy cold through my T-shirt, lashing my torso, especially after the warmth of my car's heater running at full blast.

But I don't stop, don't go back for my coat.

Not when that fucker is standing far too closely to Dommie. She backs up, opens the trunk, and starts to reach inside.

The man doesn't move, just stays right fucking there—like he's going to shove her into it, slam it closed, and drive the fuck off with her.

"...oh, thanks for the offer," Dommie is saying when I get close enough to hear the words over the brutal wind. "But it's late and I can carry my own bag."

Her tone isn't right.

Not particularly upset or tense, but...slightly slurred?

What the actual fuck?

"It's heavy and the walk is probably icy," the man says.

It's not fucking icy.

It's cold, but not icy. It hasn't snowed in weeks and—

"I'm f-fine," Dommie says, shivering.

He reaches for her backpack, takes it from her, and—

Well, fuck that.

I stop listening and start doing something.

"Thanks, man," I say, shoving between them, and snagging her bag from his hold, getting a good look at the fucker's face and hating to acknowledge that he's handsome.

Certainly, his nose is straight (read: it hasn't been broken a half dozen times like mine) and his face isn't covered with scars from sticks and pucks and fists.

A pretty, academic fucker.

I want to plant my fist into his face.

Dommie shivers again, the movement sending her wobbling.

I sling my arm around her shoulders, drawing her into my side. "Thanks for driving her home," I tell the asshole with the pretty boy face. I glance down at Dommie, see the slightly glazed eyes that tell me she had one too many glasses of wine. "Hi, baby," I say, leaning down and pressing my mouth to hers, long enough for Pretty Boy to get the message. "Let's get you inside," I say when I pull back, seeing the shock and anger and heat (because I know she feels what has my dick twitching).

"I—" she begins.

"Inside, Sunlight," I murmur, slinging her bag over my shoulder and drawing her forward.

"Dominique," the man says.

"Dommie," I correct, causing her to go still next to me.

"Dommie," he says after a moment. "Do you know this man?"

I lift my brows, want to go back to fist-planting.

But I let her answer.

And she does, after a moment. "I do, Professor Johnson," she says.

"Todd," he replies, doing some correcting of his own.

"Right." A pause. "Todd." She smiles and I tense when I see that it's a bit frazzled around the edges.

What the fuck?

But before that thought goes any further, she says, "Thank you again for the ride home."

Then she starts walking, and she's strong for her size, so she manages to draw me forward a pace. I could fight her, but because I ultimately want to get away from this asshole and into her apartment, I let her guide me up to the sidewalk and toward her front door.

"Keys," I say when we get there, a little surprised when she hands them over, but not about to look a gift horse in the mouth.

I unlock the door, push it open, wait for her to walk inside before following her.

I start to close it then pause, stare drawn back to the parking lot, to Dommie's spot which still has *Todd's—Professor fucking Johnson's*—car sitting in it.

And he's standing there next to it, staring up at us, at the open door.

Watching and waiting.

I ignore that it feels all too much like what I had been doing for the last hours and I wait and watch right back.

Wait and watch until he finally gets into his car and drives away.

Only when his sedan has disappeared from the lot do I back up enough to shut and lock the door.

I turn around and see Dommie standing there.

I expect to see her looking pissed, prepared to take a shot at me, to yell about me interfering, to order me to go.

Instead, she places a palm on the wall, kicks off one shoe and then the other.

ZIIIP!

I blink, watch her shrug off her coat, drop it to the floor.

She turns around, takes a few steps down the hall.

Stops.

Glances over her shoulder.

Our eyes connect, and I watch her lips form the question long before my mind processes the words.

"You coming?"

Ten

I can hardly believe that the words have come out of my mouth.

You coming?

You. *Coming.*

Well, hopefully both of us are going to be.

Now, I know I'm a little buzzed. I know I had one too many drinks at the faculty dinner, but the rounds kept coming and I met a group of cool people—students who are as focused as me, who have businesses on the side like me, faculty who are genuinely interested and encouraging and...

Professor Johnson.

Todd.

Who looked on with pride in his eyes.

But also—and this is the part that sent worry slicing through my insides—looked on with *possession* in his deep blue eyes.

That was what had me drinking a little too much.

Warring with myself.

I know that if I wanted to find a distraction from Walker, I could find it with Todd.

But...

I know better.

I know that Todd isn't acting appropriately. While he hasn't touched me improperly or cornered me or generally made me feel uncomfortable, he's also walking that fine line, giving rise to uneasy feelings that this could be very, very wrong.

I'm his student.

And the last hours have made me absolutely, *critically* aware that if I gave him the slightest opportunity, he would have been standing exactly where Walker is, and he wouldn't be hesitating— like Walker is—in following me down the hall to my bedroom.

I would be naked and fucked.

But...I didn't—*don't*—want him.

I want Walker.

Even if I've been fighting it.

Even if I might—*likely*—would get hurt.

So...

You coming?

I stop at my bedroom door, reach for the hem of my sweater, and yank it up and over my head, loving that I can hear his hiss from twenty feet away, all the way from the other side of my apartment, the family room and kitchen between us.

I slowly spin to face him, can feel the blistering heat of his gaze even from that distance.

It's like my skin is set on fire, scorched and reduced to ash as I reach up behind me, as I undo the hooks on the back of my bra.

I let it fall away from my chest, that blaze in his eyes causing my nipples to bead.

I'm not cold—far fucking from it.

It's just...I can feel his roughened fingertips rolling the tight nubs.

Feel the hot, wet suction of his mouth drawing them deep.

A bolt of pleasure arrows through my stomach, down to my pussy, gathering moisture between my thighs.

I reach for the button of my jeans.

"Dommie," he says, and it's a warning.

One I don't heed.

Flick.

Zip.

Down, shoving the denim past my thighs, kicking it off my calves, stepping on it—rather ungracefully because I *am* buzzed, because I'm not very graceful in general—to get it off my feet.

I step clear of the fabric and toe it to the side when I feel it.

Feel *him.*

I didn't hear him move, but suddenly he's right in front of me when I look up, the heat of his body searing my flesh nearly as much as his stare had.

"Don't," he says as my hands go to my hips, to the waistband of my underwear.

He's seen me naked.

But that's not at all what gives me confidence, what has me pushing the material down without the slightest hesitation.

It's that he clearly likes my body and has never hesitated to show me that.

He doesn't care that my stomach jiggles and is rounded, that my thigh gap is nonexistent, that while my triceps are cut and defined from all my piping, the rest of my body probably shows even more evidence of my love of the baked goods I create.

He has licked and stroked and kissed every part of me, and never did I feel anything but beautiful and wanted and—

That's why it fucking *hurt.*

I grind my teeth together, relishing the pain through my jaw, clinging to it. Because I'm buzzed and that makes me emotional. Because I'm buzzed and emotional and sure as fuck don't want to end up crying in front of this man.

I shed enough tears over him in the privacy of my bedroom, in the shower, in the dark watching late-night talk show hosts crack jokes about politicians.

Not in front of him.

Not in front of *anyone.*

Not ever again.

I inhale. Exhale silently.

And step out of the patterned material of my underwear. It's not silk, isn't lacy. It's just simple cotton. But it's soft as hell and comfortable and adorned with an adorable rainbow of stripes. I love the brand so much that I own a pair in every style and color and pattern.

But that's not what I'm focused on as I turn away again, as I crane my neck so I can watch Walker watching me, watching my ass—also nice and juicy because...baked goods.

I'm focused on the need burning in my belly and gathering between my thighs.

I'm focused on my mouth watering, desperate to get his cock inside it, to slip the thick length between my lips and swallow it so deeply that my eyes water.

I'm focused on...impending orgasms.

I tear my eyes away and flick on the light to my bedroom, blinking against the sudden brightness, but I don't stop moving until I reach the edge of my mattress, until I glance back over my shoulder again and see the stark need on display on his face.

I sit down.

Spread my thighs.

He inhales sharply.

"I need you," I murmur.

"Dommie," he says, moving toward me. "This is a bad idea."

I snake a hand down my belly, slip it between my legs, dip it into the slick heat of my pussy, groaning as I allow my fingers to go straight to my greedy clit.

Not a bad idea.

The *best* idea ever.

Even if I have to finish myself off.

Because I know how much he likes to watch me do that.

"You're drunk, Sunlight," he rasps, but he's still moving closer. "You're going to wake up in the morning and regret this."

Maybe.

But also, yeah *no*.

I let myself fall back to the mattress, spread my legs wider, circling my clit with my thumb, allowing my fingers to dip inside.

"Walker," I murmur. "Lick me."

"Fuck," he growls.

"Please," I say on a moan, my head dropping back onto the blankets. "Please fuck me with your fingers and your tongue and your cock."

"Fuck."

"Please make me come, honey."

Eleven

“Please make me come, honey.”

I love hearing her call me *honey*.

I do.

But I love hearing her beg me to make her come more.

I take another step toward her even before I realize that I'm moving, and force myself to stop.

I want to fuck her.

There's absolutely no fucking doubt of that fact.

But she's drunk.

I can't take advantage of her, not with how things are between us.

We're nowhere near feeling comfortable enough with each other to have drunk sex.

Though, considering how explosive things are between us normally, adding alcohol and even fewer inhibitions and I have no doubt it'll be off the fucking charts.

“Walker,” Dommie moans, that cunt glistening with the evidence of her desire, the slick sounds of her fingers sliding in and out of her pussy the sexiest fucking thing I've ever heard. "I need you."

"I want to give it to you, baby," I say, inching closer, able to scent the tart evidence of her desire on the air. "But you'll hate me in the morning."

And I can't have that.

I fucking *can't*.

"I won't," she says. "I promise you that I won't."

Which is a lie—even if she doesn't think so right now. "Baby," I begin.

Her hips arch up toward me, and I take another step, close enough that my hand lands on top of her knee.

Silky skin.

So fucking tempting to touch, to stroke up along the insides of her thighs, to get my fingers into that cunt.

But—

She lifts her leg, resting her foot on the edge of the mattress.

And...look at that...my hand slides along her thigh, drifts close to her pussy.

Near enough that I can feel her desire coating the tops of her legs, so close that my fingers get trapped in the crease of her thighs, get knocked toward that slick heat as she works herself, as she moans, head digging into the bed, pelvis rocking.

She's close.

I've tasted her orgasm as she falls apart, tasted it on her flesh, had the gush of her desire coating my tongue, dripping down my beard. I've tasted it on her lips, her groans of pleasure mingling with mine. I've felt that pussy clenching around my fingers, my cock.

But my favorite?

This.

Watching her come apart, those slender fingers working herself.

I can see her labia go pink and grow plump, can see them glisten in the light of the fixture overhead.

I can see the way her toes curl as she gets close, her tits bounce as her hand works furiously.

I can see the blush spread over her chest, up her throat, to the tops of her cheeks.

Eyes closed tight, lips parted, breaths coming rapidly.

And the best?

When she's right there and I can't contain myself any longer.

I reach in, brushing her fingers aside, causing her lids to fly open, a protest forming on her tongue. But I'm already moving, already giving in, already giving her exactly what she wants.

I don't know why I bothered to deny her.

The whole fucking world could be looking on and I would still be giving her everything that she asks for.

I press her clit hard, just the way she likes it, spearing two fingers deep inside.

"Walker!"

That's fucking perfect, like a palm trailing down my chest, dipping beneath the waistband of my jeans, slipping into my underwear, and wrapping a hand around my cock.

Stroking it hard and fast and without mercy.

Sending me close to an edge I shouldn't be at, considering I'm fully clothed and not doing this.

Only, I'm fully clothed and I *am* doing this.

Fucking her with my fingers, circling her clit, working that bundle of nerves exactly as she likes—confidently and a little rough and not stopping, even when she begs me to.

Because she needs help getting over the edge.

Because she gets so fucking sensitized that—

I shove another finger deep, lean forward and suck one pouty nipple into my mouth, pulling on it harder than I normally would —except that I know she needs that roughness, the pressure, the hint of teeth on the sensitive bud.

Her hands come to my head, short nails biting into my scalp.

I growl, suck deeper, move my fingers faster, grasp tightly to my control, fighting to not pull back, unzip and shove my pants down.

To not plunge into the slick heat of her, to feel that pussy clenching my dick.

Not today.

Give her this.

But that's all until we can talk—

"Oh!" she gasps, grip on my hair growing fiercer. It sends darts of pain through my nerves, but I don't give a fuck because I can feel *it*.

The flutters of her pussy.

The beginnings of her orgasm.

There's a gush of liquid coating my fingers, and she moans again, louder and deeper than before. The evidence of her desire drips out, covering my palm, easing my path.

It would be so easy to slip inside.

To slip *my cock* inside.

But I don't.

I just keep stroking her as she catapults up that peak, as she hovers right there on the precipice, as though her body is waiting for permission to come.

I bite down on her nipple.

"*Oh!*" she moans. "Oh my fucking God!"

Her pussy clamps down on my fingers, and...she's gone.

Coming apart as she flies over the edge. Her grip tightens further for several heartbeats, her entire body tensing beneath mine, but then she's relaxing, then she's slumping to the bed, hands sliding free of my hair, limbs going lax underneath me.

My dick is hard, pushing against my zipper, desperate to be inside that slick pussy of hers.

But I manage to keep control, manage to coax her down from the edge, to ease her landing back onto Earth.

And then I straighten, pull back, opening my mouth to tell her that we have to stop here, that we can't go any further—

Snore!

I look down, see her eyes closed, her breaths slow and steady. And realize that she's fallen asleep.

Twelve

Dommie

BEEP! BEEP! BEEP!

I groan, not wanting to open my eyes because I'm warm and cozy and have the slightest bit of a headache beginning at my temples.

I don't want to get up and drag around heavy containers of ingredients, don't want to hear the whirring of the mixers going at full speed.

I just want to sleep off the one too many glasses of wine and—

Wine.

Professor Johnson.

Todd.

Walker.

And me stripping naked and begging him to make me come.

Not one too many glasses of wine.

About an infinite too many.

My eyes fly open and I'm nose-to-nose with a big, broad chest.

"Oh my fucking God," I mutter, trying to extricate myself from Walker's hold.

BEEP! BEEP! BEEP!

I try harder, desperate now to silence the alarm before he wakes up, to escape (even though it's my apartment and I really don't have anywhere to escape to, considering he's fucking sleeping in my bed), but the arm around my back, the arm that is keeping me plastered against that big, warm, BROAD chest just tightens, locking me in place.

BEEP! BEEP! BEEP!

Shit. Shit. *Shit.*

I struggle now, deciding that crocodile death rolling may be necessary in order to facilitate my escape, even if it means waking the beast.

I'll just hide in the bathroom until he falls back asleep or gives up.

Because both of those are likely.

Sure.

Of course they are.

BEEP! BEEP! BEEP!

I grunt and shove both hands against Walker's chest, putting all of my strength into my push, managing to gain all of a couple of inches.

But it's enough for me to wriggle out of Walker's hold, to make an escape attempt.

Only, just as I reach the edge of the bed, my feet heading for the carpet below, an arm wraps around my middle—

"*Oof!*" I grunt, and a second later, I'm back against that big, broad chest.

"Where the fuck do you think you're going, Sunlight?" Walker says, voice a mix of sleepy and grumpy, and it rasps along my skin, dips between my thighs, exactly as his fingers did last night—

BEEP! BEEP! BEEP!

"I need to turn off my alarm before my neighbors complain," I say, ignoring that I'm suddenly breathless.

"Such a beautiful little liar," he murmurs, not releasing me, although he does reach over and turn off my alarm so I don't have to hear the annoying ass *BEEP! BEEP! BEEP!* again.

"I'm not a liar," I mutter.

"Baby," he says, dropping his hand to the mattress next to me, forearms boxing me in, heavy weight of his body settling in the cradle of my thighs.

I wait for him to say something else, maybe to call me a liar again, maybe to comment on my antics the night before, but he doesn't do either.

And he doesn't have to, I suppose.

He just looks at me with his chocolate-brown eyes and waits.

"You're probably mad that I didn't show up for dinner yesterday," I begin.

His head tilts to the side, and the barest hint of a smile curves his lips. "No, Sunlight, I knew you'd do anything in your power to avoid that dinner."

"Oh," I say, some part of me strangely disappointed.

He knew I wasn't going to come?

And he was just going to...give up on me?

After all that talk at the bakery?

Why is that strangely disappointing?

It shouldn't be.

But...

It is.

Damn.

His brows flick up, as though he can see that inner battle. "Which is why I showed up here to wait for you at four o'clock," he murmurs, lips brushing along my jaw.

Now *my* brows flick up. "At four?" I ask softly.

"Yup," he says, straightening. "I never underestimate you, baby. Though"—his mouth curves further—"I *did* expect you to either come home and not answer the doorbell, or to come home and then go stay at Eva's."

"I couldn't go to Eva's," I admit despite the fact that it's stupid to reveal I *had* thought about doing that, to give him more ammunition to use against me.

More ammunition than stripping myself naked and begging him to fuck me?

Right. Probably not.

I ignore that, grind my back teeth together, shut the fuck up, push last night away, and try to wait him out.

"No," he says, "I realized that after five thirty had come and gone. If you went to Eva and Theo's, they would just let me in. So then I figured you either stayed out studying—hence me hanging in the parking lot, intending to catch you on your way in—or had deployed *Mission Impossible* skills to sneak inside your apartment."

He's funny.

Damn. Why does he have to be funny?

"Oh," I say softly.

Fingers on my cheek. "So, where were you?"

"What?"

"Well," he murmurs, shifting his weight slightly, sliding his hand down and cupping the side of my neck, "you weren't playing secret agent and I don't think you came home drunk after spending hours in the library, so...where were you?"

I inhale, part of me not wanting to tell him, just because I'm feeling vulnerable and recalcitrant and don't *want* to tell him.

Stubborn Moreno DNA coming to the forefront.

The rest of me...wants to share.

Because last night had been...

Exciting.

Not spending time with Professor Johnson, though he's a very smart man and the invite had been a really nice gesture, but it was the dinner as a whole. The conversation. The teachers and other students, being amongst a group of people who were excited to learn. Who have big ideas and weren't scared to kick ass and—

"I went to a faculty dinner," I say quietly. "Professor Johnson invited me."

"Todd," he mutters.

I ignore the slice of irritation in his tone. "They have it quarterly," I tell him. "A bunch of faculty members get together with students they see are excelling. They eat and drink and talk and —" I exhale, remembering how good it felt to be included in that group. "It was nice to have a night like that."

"He drive anyone else home?"

My nostrils flare, annoyance flaring. "What does that matter?"

Walker drops his head a little closer, his breath coating my lips. "It matters."

I look away, reconsider that crocodile death rolling.

"You can try it"—my gaze flashes back to see him smirking—"but know I'd really like feeling your body writhing beneath mine."

I wrinkle my nose even though I know I'd really like it too. "Pig."

One shoulder lifts toward his ear, drops. "Maybe. But I'm also not the one who was begging to get fucked last night."

I shove at his chest. "Asshole."

A grin. "Yup." He brushes his mouth over mine. "And *Todd* didn't drive anyone home," Walker says. "I know he didn't because no man looks at a woman like he looked at you and drove other people home."

I scowl. "How did he look at me?"

"Like he wants to fuck you." A scowl of his own.

"That's not why he drove me home," I say.

Another shrug. "Maybe. Maybe not. But he wasn't going to turn down a chance to get in your pants."

I know this.

I also don't want to admit it, not when Walker is looking so fucking proud of himself for knowing it too.

"I need to get up," I say instead. "I have to get to the bakery."

His hand slides to my cheek. "Still such a beautiful little liar," he says, causing my heart to skip a beat.

"I'm not lying." I'm not—or not about this, anyway. I have to work this morning.

"Oh no, Sunlight," he tells me, his hand skating down, drifting along my neck, moving further south. I almost startle when I realize it's dragging over fabric.

Last I remember, I was naked.

But now—my eyes flick down—I see I'm wearing Walker's T-shirt.

That explains the scent of him all around me.

"I know you're not lying about working this morning," he says, drawing my focus back to him, "but you don't have to leave for another hour."

His hand slides lower.

"And I have a really great idea about what to do with that time."

THIRTEEN

WALKER

Her eyes go wide as I bend further, as I give in to the urge I've had from the moment she woke up.

To kiss her.

Fuck morning breath.

Fuck the distance she keeps trying to put between us.

Fuck my *reasons*.

She's beneath me.

She's sober.

She—

My lips hit hers and...

Explosion.

Of sensation—the softness of her lips, the floral, sweet, baked-good scent that is inherently Dommie, the way her body gives to mine, curves lush and accepting.

Of desire—electricity sparking through my veins, need coiling in my abdomen, my cock going rock-hard in an instant.

Of affection—for the quiet moan that escapes her mouth when I break away, kissing my way along her jaw, pausing at the sensitive spot just beneath it, the one that never fails to make her melt, to make her sigh out my name.

More.

I move my hand along her side, dragging it over the curve of her breast, the indent of her waist, the flare of her hip.

And then I make it to the hem of my T-shirt.

And the silky skin beneath.

"Walker," she murmurs, but it's not a protest.

In fact, her thighs part and one leg hitches over my hip, her heel digging into my ass. She rocks against me, grinds that bare pussy against my jeans that I didn't trust myself to take off.

Jeans that are getting tighter and more uncomfortable by the moment.

"Sunlight," I murmur back, allowing my hand to drift up, this time beneath the cotton, moving toward her breasts, toward the nipples I fucking love to suck.

"*Walker,*" she moans as I pinch one.

Not gentle. Not coaxing.

We don't have time for that.

She has gorgeous pastries to make, cakes to decorate, cookies to ice.

But I'm going to make her come before she has to go do that.

I nip at her throat, roll that taut bud between thumb and forefinger as she grinds against me, as my dick somehow gets harder, and I ride a dangerous edge between letting her continue and unzipping and plunging inside that wet ass pussy.

But...*reasons.*

I rear back, dislodging her leg as I reach for the hem of my shirt covering her, as I yank it up and over her head, making those gorgeous tits bounce. I let it fly, not giving a fuck where it lands, then wrap my arm around her middle and flip her over so that gorgeous ass is in the air.

She gasps.

I run my hand along the bumps of her spine then swat my palm across the lush curve of one cheek.

Another gasp, but she arches that ass up, silently asking for the spanking I desperately want to dish out. "As much as I want to worship this ass, Sunlight," I murmur. "You have a bakery to run." I dip my fingers down before she can protest, sliding them through the crease there, pressing lightly against the taut entrance I want to lick, to fuck with my fingers and tongue and cock.

But...

Bakery.

So, I allow them to continue sliding, to slip into the hot, slick heat of her cunt.

And hear her gasp, feel the clamp of her muscles around my fingers, know that I'm not going to be able to resist the temptation of her pussy this time.

"Ready, baby?" I rasp, fucking her with my fingers slow and steady and deep.

"Inside me," she orders, rocking her hips back, fucking my hand, grinding against me. "*Now*, Walker."

I'm tempted to make both of us wait, just because.

But...bakery.

So I keep my fingers moving inside her as I reach over her body, snag my wallet from the nightstand.

I keep my fingers moving inside her as I extract a condom and tear it open with my teeth.

As I manage to pull out the latex sheath and roll it down the length of my erection.

As I notch the head of my cock at her entrance.

And push in, trapping my fingers inside, feeling her squirm against me.

"Too much?" I ask, wrapping my other hand around her hip, sliding out, thrusting in. Fingers and cock. Fingers and cock. Fingers and—

Her pussy flutters, clamps hard around me.

Her ass tips up, hips starting to rock back, fast and furious.

And...my orgasm is suddenly right fucking *there*.

"Sunlight," I rasp, trying to halt her movements, to stop her before she sends me over the edge.

But she's either super strong or I'm not trying all that hard to slow her down.

She slides forward and back, that cunt tight around me.

And I lose patience, pulling my slick fingers from her heat, wrapping them around her other hip, gripping both sides of her waist so I have control and can fuck her as hard, as fast, as furious as she's fucking me.

It's glorious, fucking beautiful, fucking incredible...

Fucking—

There.

Me. Her.

That pussy convulsing as she topples over the edge.

My vision hazes, red creeping in around the perimeter, reducing the room to just this woman, to my dick parting her slick folds and disappearing into that tight cunt.

My orgasm gathers at the base of my spine for one long moment.

Then I explode, coming harder than I've ever before as I stroke into her once, twice, three more times.

"Fuck," I groan as I collapse forward, as I manage to pull enough of myself together to roll us to our sides so I don't crush her. My chest is heaving. My back is covered in sweat. I don't want either of us to move for a hundred years—

BEEP! BEEP! BEEP!

But...

Bakery.

I groan as I summon enough energy to snag her cell, to turn off the alarm, apparently not having done it properly the first time. Then I toss her phone back onto the nightstand and flop back, gathering her close.

My dick is still hard.

More than ready to have a second, a third, a fourth round.

But...

Bakery.

So, I just hold her tight for a moment, critically aware that even as her breathing slows, as she, no doubt, drifts back to Earth, she doesn't say anything.

That she just lays silently in the circle of my arms.

Fourteen

Dommie

He's holding me like I mean something.

Like I'm precious and valuable and *important*.

And look, I'm not saying that I need a man to hold me close, to cradle me against his chest, for his palm and fingers to rub lightly over my stomach to my hip and then back to my stomach, tracing nonsensical patterns on my skin...

It's just...when he touches me like this...

I *feel* important.

And valuable.

And *more*.

So much more that it crawls under my skin like ants, prickling, uncomfortable, too fucking intense.

So intense that my lungs seize, that panic wells up in my throat.

Making it almost impossible for me to breathe, to think, to not run screaming from the room.

"Easy, Sunlight," Walker says softly, that hand sliding up the middle of my chest, pressing lightly. "Easy now," he says. "In and out. Just *in and out*." Maybe it should make things worse, the orders, his palm sitting where my lungs feel the most tight, the pressure. But...it doesn't.

It's like that hand is my lodestone.

I inhale, hold it for the count of three.

Then exhale, slow and steady, until my lungs feel empty.

"Good, baby," he murmurs. "That's good. That's perfect. That's—"

"I need to go," I whisper.

"Yeah," he says. But he doesn't move that hand from between my breasts as he sits up, as the blanket slides down my body, the cold morning air clinging to my skin. He doesn't move it as he shifts us to the edge of the bed, as he swings our legs over, as he stands.

Then it shifts, sliding as he wraps his arm around me, as he lifts me up and strides to my bathroom.

I blink when he flicks on the light.

And I melt when he pauses to spread a towel on the vanity's counter before setting me on top of it.

While I'm trying not to turn into a puddle, he turns away, cranks on the shower.

Then cups my cheek, turns my face back to him. "Coffee?"

My teeth in my bottom lip. My cheeks feeling hot.

My belly fluttering.

But then I nod.

His hand slides down to my jaw, tilting my face up so he can stare into my eyes. "I'm taking you to dinner tonight."

I shake my head. "You have a game tonight."

One big shoulder lifting and falling. "So, we'll go to dinner early."

More butterflies, but I ignore them. "I have to deliver a wedding cake."

His mouth quirks. "So, I'll come with you. Give Roy the afternoon off."

Roy.

How the fuck does he know who Roy is?

"Work for you, Sunlight?" he asks.

I narrow my eyes. "You're *asking* now?"

That mouth quirks further. "I can make it an order if you want."

Despite the fact that I need to keep my distance from this man, that I really shouldn't be amused by his antics because he's dangerous for my heart, for my mental well-being, I feel something inside me soften.

I inhale, long and deep, try to harden it back up.

But it melts like butter in a hot pan.

"We'll deliver the cake," he says. "I'll feed you. Then you can come to the game." His fingers squeeze. "I know you like to sit in the stands, so I'll spare you the family suite."

I haven't been to a Breakers game in what feels like forever.

It's not that Eva and Theo haven't offered.

They have.

But I'm always busy with work and school and...

Avoiding a certain hockey player.

Who has just fucked me senseless and is currently gently cupping the side of my neck.

Gently. *Cupping.*

And that gentle touch is what melted me before, that made me feel—

Enough.

"Work for you, Sunlight?" he asks again.

It's dumb. Beyond fucking *dumb.*

But I nod.

His expression warms and he squeezes his hand lightly before sliding it down my throat, pausing to rest it on my chest—just above my heart—for a moment.

My pulse speeds up.

"So fucking pretty," he murmurs, brushing his lips over my forehead, sending my pulse skittering even faster.

Then his hands are dropping to my waist and he's lifting me off the counter, settling my feet on the carpet. He waits a minute, as though steadying me—and my pulse is absolutely pounding now—before stepping back, turning toward the shower curtain and pulling it to the side.

I frown.

And then I understand as he puts his hand under the water.

Testing the temperature.

He adjusts the taps.

My pulse is thundering in my ears now, the warmth in my belly growing, expanding as he rotates back to face me, shaking the droplets from his hand. "Shower, baby," he murmurs, nudging me toward the tub. "I'll be back with coffee."

"I—" I bite the inside of my cheek. "Okay," I whisper.

A light swat to my ass. "Go on, Sunlight."

I move toward the tub, step over the edge—

His hand takes my arm, the other resting on my back.

Making sure I don't fall as I get in.

Fuck.

If there's a moment where I know I'm going to lose this battle, lose this war within myself (even *if* I tried to pretend the orgasms of the last twenty-four hours hadn't happened), then the way his palm flattens lightly on my back as I step into the stream of water would be it.

This man is a hurricane barreling down on me.

I can run, can flee.

But I'm still going to be trapped in the rainbands.

Then I'm fully in the shower and he's gone, leaving me standing under the warm jets of water—not too hot, not too cold —the bathroom door *clicking* softly closed.

I'm tense as I soap up, listening.

Waiting.

For him to come back. Maybe for him to join me. For him...to wrap his arms around me and hold me close forever.

He doesn't.

Not as I rinse the suds off.

Not as I shampoo and rinse, as I condition, wait the requisite five (*cough,* two, since I'm impatient) minutes and rinse again.

Not as I turn the water off.

Not as I dry myself with a towel he's left hanging over the shower rod—and I know it must have been Walker because I never remember to hang one up, because I always have to climb out of the tub, shivering as I yank the length of cotton off the towel bar and wrap it around myself.

I pull the curtain wide and carefully step out.

And I see that I'm wrong.

He *has* come back.

A steaming cup of coffee is sitting on the counter.

And alongside it is a square of my homemade protein breakfast bar.

I exhale, pick up the mug, and take a careful sip.

But I already know—and the sip confirms it—that it's going to be perfect, that it's going to be exactly as I make it for myself.

I close my eyes, hang my head, and know—

I should just wave the white flag now.

FIFTEEN

Walker

I click off from the call after ensuring that Dommie's ticket will be waiting for her at the box office, and sit in the driver's seat with my engine running, watching for her to come out of her apartment and get into her car.

And she does, right on time.

Responsible.

Follows through.

Always.

Must be a Moreno trait—or a Moreno female trait...or maybe just a Dommie and Eva trait.

Growing up they had to develop those follow-through skills.

Because their parents hadn't—or *didn't*, in the case of their mother.

There's love there from Dommie—for her siblings, of course, but also for their mother, despite the Moreno matriarch being a total bitch.

A user.

Just plain mean.

To the people she's supposed to love the most.

Carmen Moreno is one of the most unpleasant people I've ever had the displeasure of meeting.

And she's the mom of the woman I want.

Fun fucking times.

The only saving grace is that Carmen has lost all of her easy targets.

Starting with Eva moving out. Then Dommie and Gabe, and now that Jer has graduated high school and is off working his way through a gap year of travel and odd jobs and decimating the female population wherever he lands for a short amount of time, Dommie's mother no longer has the same grasp on her daughters as she once had.

They still pay for her expenses.

Not that the bitch deserves it.

Same as she doesn't deserve having them accompany her to appointments or be there for a surgery.

But Dommie and Eva do it anyway.

The only consolation is that Theo put his foot down.

They aren't alone with her.

Not ever.

Not *fucking* ever.

Theo hired several full-time nurses to go along with them—and it's those women's jobs to protect the vulnerable streak that Eva and Dommie struggle to keep safe from their mother.

They've seen the light. They know what their mother is.

But...it's not easy to leave a parent behind.

God, do I know that.

Thankfully, Eva and Dommie have erected some distance and are the better for it.

Any idiot (read: *me*) can see that much.

And they have the team on their side, starting with Theo, who's fucking smart and stubborn—stubborn enough to deal with a stubborn Moreno, and by *deal*, I mean is able to out-stubborn his wife on albeit infrequent, but important, occasions.

I've been taking notes.

Because I have my eye on my own stubborn Moreno.

She gets in her car—and I owe Theo and Eva a favor for picking it up from the university and driving it over—and backs out of her spot. I don't miss that she clocks me sitting in my car, her eyes meeting mine as she drives by.

I wink and she shakes her head slightly.

But her lips are curved.

And I'll take that.

I'll fucking take *that*.

Then her car is gone, and I have nothing keeping me in this apartment complex, not any longer anyway.

Though, I know the moment she's back here, I'll be here too.

———

The cold is dusting over my nose and cheeks as I make my way into the bakery.

I know a lot of the guys hate the snow—shoveling it off sidewalks, scraping it off windows, shitty roads, and delayed travel—but I don't mind it.

Reminds me of home.

Of the few good times.

Getting up at dawn to spend the day skiing—a splurge my mom pinched pennies to make happen a couple of times per season.

Before everything changed.

Before *she* changed.

And I—

The bell tinkles overhead and I blink, shoving the memories away, reminding myself that the shit from my past is long done with.

"Can I—?" My gaze flashes to the counter and the girl—Sonya, Dommie said her name is—smiles at me then tilts her head toward the back of the bakery. "She's in the kitchen."

Probably because I've made the same walk—rounding the counter, slipping by the refrigerated case of delectable treats, pushing through the swinging metal doors that separate the kitchen from the front of the house more than a few times.

"Thanks," I say as I make that trek.

She smiles and then I'm moving into the warm and sweet-smelling kitchen, feeling something settling in me as I see Dommie standing at the counter, her sleek brown hair tied back into a ponytail.

She looks up at me, eyes narrowing slightly.

But it's not full-scowl, and I don't miss that her coffee-colored irises are warm. Tentative, a little shy, but not full of the rage I had previously earned.

Not full of the hurt I had been responsible for putting there.

I exhale and move a little closer—

Okay, fine.

I move a *lot* closer, not stopping until I'm side-by-side with her.

She lifts the piping bag from the cookie she's decorating, and though I've eaten Eva's cookies, seen that our broadcaster has some skill with decorating, I understand in an instant that it's nowhere near her sister's. Dommie's has this...effortless charm. Clean lines and even layers, each design identical, even though there has to be a hundred cookies on the stainless steel table.

Eva is talented.

Dommie has that talent sewn into her soul.

I reach up, wipe at her cheek, some part of me deep inside loving when her eyes warm, when her body melts just slightly, drifting toward mine.

"What is it?" she whispers.

"You have frosting on your cheek."

She flushes and starts to look away, but I capture her jaw, catching it in the palm of my hand.

"So fucking pretty," I murmur.

Her inhale is sharp and her body wavers closer.

I want to kiss her.

I want to show her that I mean those words to the very depths of my soul.

But there are a hundred cookies—at least—on the table, and we have a wedding cake to deliver, and...

She's not ready.

I step away from her, putting some distance between us before I do something that will result in dozens of cookie deaths. "I'll pull my car around to the back while you finish those." I might be drawn to her like a moth to the flame, might want to yank her jeans down before lifting her, settling her on the table, scattering those beautiful works of art as I part her legs, kneel between them, and taste her orgasm on my tongue...but I can't have her.

Not right now.

Because that would involve sending her cookies toppling to the tile floor, destroying that art, decimating her hard work.

And I've hurt her enough already.

But I can't resist brushing my lips over hers, the feather-like touch lasting barely longer than a heartbeat.

Because if I allow myself anything more than that, those cookies will be on the floor.

I wrap my fingers around her wrist, lift her hand—the one with the piping bag—and order softly, "Finish your cookies, Sunlight. I'll be right back."

A shaky exhale.

But then she nods and pulls gently out of my hold, rolling her shoulders as she brings the metal tip of the piping bag toward a cookie, one of the few remaining to be decorated.

I watch her for a long moment.

Graceful. Confident. The fucking center of my universe.

Then she lifts her head, meets my eyes, and my heart rolls over in my chest when half of her mouth curves. "I thought you were going to move your car around so we can load the cake up."

I blink, shake my head.

Then smile sheepishly back at her.

Then I go and move my car around to the back of the bakery.

Sixteen

Dommie

He's propping up a wall at the wedding venue, watching me work after being nothing but my lackey for the last couple of hours.

First, to place cookies on trays that he then slid neatly onto the upright rack I have in one corner of the bakery's kitchen so they can dry properly over the next twenty-four hours.

Sonya will bag them tomorrow, and then they'll be shipped off for a bridal shower happening a few states away.

Then to help me finish boxing the cakes and place them in their special transport carriers so they wouldn't be damaged in transit.

Then to help me lug the layers inside the venue, to carry the loose decorations I need to put the finishing touches on the cake.

Which is what I'm currently doing.

After having painstakingly stacked the layers and piped tiny beads of frosting to hide the seams.

Now, I'm placing stray sugar pearls with tweezers and blowing edible glitter off the tip of a tiny paintbrush, scattering it in perfect arcs of glimmering goodness.

Everything is better with glitter.

Everything.

I glance over my shoulder for the umpteenth time, lips curving when I think about Walker bitching regularly about glitter being craft herpes—and how I purposely picked a very special wrapping paper for his present at Christmas dinner. Maybe that won't make sense to other people, buying something for a man who hurt me, who I chose to be furious with because if I allowed myself to really study my true feelings, they would reveal too much, would reveal how I still *felt* too much. But, feelings or not, my sister wanted a family dinner, and that family of hers and Theo's included my siblings, Theo's sisters and his mom and step-dad, and...Walker.

Who I might have wanted to skewer with a thousand tiny toothpicks, but I wouldn't.

Because that dinner was critically important to my sister.

So, I played nice...within reason.

And wrapping his present in the most glittery wrapping paper of all wrapping paper was within reason.

So much glitter.

(And maybe some *inside* the wrapping paper as well).

And...a new nickname was born.

Heh.

He pushes off the wall, crossing over to me, eyes curious when he leans close and rumbles, "What, Sunlight?"

Mischief takes over—that's the only explanation for what I do next.

Which is lifting that paintbrush toward his beard...

And blowing sharply.

Flecks of glitter fly through the air...

And catch in the strands of his beard.

Heat in his deep brown eyes, and payback, but there isn't anger. Just...a promise of retribution. "You're playing a dangerous game, baby," he murmurs, one big, warm hand settling on my hip. His fingers flex. "A *very* dangerous game."

"I think that silver adds a certain…" I tilt my head to the side, considering. "*Je ne sais quoi.*" A beat because I'm enjoying this, because I'm revealing in being part of something now integral to the Breakers family—Walker's new nickname. "It looks good, *Glitter.*"

His big chest expands, brows lifting, the promise of payback growing in his expression—albeit still without a lick of anger. Instead, it's a dark amusement that has dampness gathering at the apex of my thighs. "You itching for payback, baby?"

I shiver.

Because I can think of several versions of *payback* he can give me—and they all have very pleasurable ends.

Not that I tell him that. Instead, I lift my chin and tease, "My glitter-laden wrapping paper is the shit."

Glitter just isn't a fan.

Case in point? The way he scowls at me.

I grin. "And you're just salty because tonight's Walker Laine bobblehead night."

He scowls and rubs a hand over his beard, scattering the sparkling flecks, and making my grin grow. The thick, dark strands will be represented in glitter-covered form on the tiny head-bobbing dolls given out to fans tonight. "Fucking media team," he grumbles. "I'd forgotten they were doing that."

"Oh," I say lightly. "I thought that's why you wanted me to come tonight." I giggle. "So I can get the souvenir I inspired."

Those deep brown eyes narrow—more danger, more intangible punishments coming my way.

"And *now* you're playing with fire," he rumbles, hand skating down my spine, body drifting closer.

I want to lean into him, to step into those flames, to allow them to dance over my skin.

He'll protect me from the blistering heat.

Or maybe…he'll allow us both to play inside the blaze.

But…later.

I force myself to turn back to the cake, surveying it carefully, trying to spot any areas that need fixing or more glitter or a white gum paste flower.

It's perfect—or as perfect as it's going to get.

I know if I keep fiddling and adding and tweaking, it's going to look worse.

And anyway, Walker needs to get to the arena.

So, I tear myself away from further fussing, start packing up the extra supplies and my tools. To his credit, Walker doesn't push his point, just starts carrying out the boxes I pack up, disappearing through the side door of the glassed, indoor garden space. It's a gorgeous location, the slightly humid interior having required me to get creative with decorations.

No melting cakes on my watch.

Or gum paste flowers detaching and falling to the ground.

Luckily the cake table is on wheels and will be rolled from the temperature-controlled kitchen out into the garden space much closer to cutting time.

Otherwise...full melt.

Because they'd have to pay me a lot more than what they are in order for me to deliver a cake at eight o'clock at night.

Tomorrow is Saturday.

The absolute busiest day at the bakery.

I'll be up at the crack of dawn, and I'm already pushing it with the hockey game—pushing it doing something I *want* to be doing, no matter how stupid that is.

I don't want to stay up late on bakery business.

I want to spend time with Walker. Despite his *reasons*.

There.

I'm admitting it.

Which is why after he drops me back at the bakery—and helps me unload my boxes, *and* gently cups my jaw before brushing his lips over mine, I don't go and lock myself in the walk-in, hiding from what I want and how it scares me.

It's why, even though I'll likely end up with a twice-broken heart, I hang up my apron and drive back to my apartment.

Because when I close my eyes at night, I dream of him.

Long for more from him.

Wish he's next to me, that he's holding me and kissing me and...

I miss just talking, how he studies me closely when I speak, as though he doesn't want to chance not hearing a single word.

I miss...how he made me feel important and valued and—

"*More*," I whisper, tugging my Breakers jersey over my head, allowing it to fall over my long-sleeved thermal. It has Theo's— and Eva's new—last name, Young, on the back and because it's a game-worn jersey, it's huge, hanging to mid-thigh and requiring me to get creative with my tucking.

Thanks, TikTok's hair tie trick.

A sacrificial elastic. A couple of twists. And then the material isn't engulfing me any longer.

I look in the mirror, know that my boyfriend jeans, Converse, light makeup, and hair down in slightly uneven waves is as good as it's going to get.

If Walker wants a supermodel, he's going to have to keep looking.

Like he had before.

Moving on to a slender blonde, who was tall enough, beautiful enough to match him.

Not a curvy hobbit who gets eaten by hockey jerseys and often wears frosting on my cheek.

My heart pulses, remembering how much it hurt when I saw them together, when I came to understand what those *reasons* he keeps mentioning were.

He wanted someone else, even if he isn't cruel enough to tell me that straight out.

And now he's back and I'm a glutton for punishment and I'm going to soak in every moment that he'll give me.

He made me feel more...

Until he made me feel less.

"Stupid," I whisper on a heavy sigh. "So *damned* stupid."

I narrow my eyes, but it doesn't change the fact that it's true, and that I'm doing this anyway.

Soaking up life, even when it'll bite back.

I turn away from my reflection.

And I drive to the arena.

SEVENTEEN

I look for her during warm-ups, knowing exactly what seat she's supposed to be in.

But it's empty the entire time both of our teams are skating circles and handling pucks and going through the motions of whatever good luck, warm-up rituals each of us have.

Sometimes it's being on the ice first.

Sometimes it's doing a certain sequence of stretches.

Sometimes it's stick-handling—toe to heel, backhand to forehand, tracing patterns on the ice, warming up wrists around a logo beneath the surface of the rink.

Sometimes it's a certain shot that needs to be made—this being mine.

I have to shoot the puck once over the top of the net (above the right corner, if I'm being specific) for it to be a good game.

Just once.

More than that? I'm fucked.

I miss out on doing it? Also, fucked.

Today, though, I do it first thing, ticking it off my to-do list before I give in and allow my gaze to drift up into the stands, past the people clustered at the glass, knowing I'll be unfocused as shit until the puck drops.

Once that happens, the rest of the world falls away.

It's just skating hard and hitting motherfuckers on the other team. Threading passes through legs and over stick blades and, hopefully, into the goal.

It's bantering on the bench and listening to Coach talk—and sometimes yell.

It's feeling the high when I score and then having that high get even higher when it's my teammates putting the puck in the net.

But puck properly sent over the goal or not, I don't feel high right then.

Because Dommie's seat is empty.

Because Dommie might have decided not to come. I can't blame her for that, not after what I did, how I handled things, the *reasons* I haven't shared with her.

She would be smart not to—

Bang. Bang. Bang!

I jerk my head up from where I was stretching near the boards, gaze going to the commotion on the far side of the ice.

My heart leaps when I spot a woman with familiar light brown hair standing at the glass, a wide smile on her face as she gestures...

To someone next to her.

A growl rises in my throat as I rip my stare from hers, jerk it to the right, and—

Oh.

Oh.

She points to the sign and I find my lips curving up as I skate across the ice, nearly getting plowed down by Jackson, who's doing his random ass skating drill warmup that looks ridiculous, but he swears is integral to his game.

I don't see how swizzles and alternating C-cuts help with that, but I shoot to miss in order to play better, so who the fuck am I to judge?

And Jackson has been playing his ass off, has been one of the team's leading scorers, so—again—no judging coming from my direction.

Plus, I'm lucky that one of his C-cuts sends him out of my way, though he narrows his eyes at me as he makes the maneuver.

No doubt, I'll get him growling at me again.

Whatever.

The worry about that is dropped almost immediately, probably because dodging Jackson—or him dodging me, anyway—brings me within a couple of feet of the boards.

Close enough to get a good look at Dommie, and the person next to her.

The *kid* next to her.

A skinny boy with floppy brown hair, a mouth that's dropped open, eyes gone wide. He's clutching a small poster board and—

Damn.

Fingers wrapping around my heart, squeezing tight.

The sign reads,

I beat cancer! You can beat the Eagles!

Christ.

Kids are my fucking weak spot. And kids who are innocent and go through bad shit and somehow come through the other side smiling, like this kid is—now that he's processed I'm there for him—can tear me wide open.

Can lay me right the fuck out at center ice.

Dommie touches the boy's shoulder, having him spin around, showing me the back of his jersey.

Laine sewn at the top. My number—38—situated below it.

Christ.

It's like fingers have wrapped around my heart and squeezed tight.

It's why, those months ago, when those *reasons* showed up on my doorstep, I—

I slam the wall down on those memories. It's all over. I know the truth, and *reasons* have moved on, searching for their next mark.

The kid turns back around, and I pose for a pic as well as I can through the glass before I bend down and scoop up a puck, tossing it over the boards. He clutches it close, his smile so wide it seems at risk of splitting his face wide open.

Dommie is smiling nearly as wide as she lifts her palm up for him to high-five, but in turning to offer her hand to the kid, she gives me a glimpse of her back.

And it's not my fucking name on that jersey she's wearing.

Some part of me knows it's impossible for it to be—that I haven't given her one with my name, haven't treated her in a way that meant she would want to buy one herself.

The rest of my possessive, animalistic, tiny little caveman brain buries that logic as jealousy burns through me. I want to bust through the glass and tear off Theo's name, want to rip the fabric over her head and replace it with my own.

I want to—

The buzzer goes and I manage to get it together, to hide the scalding emotions I'm feeling deeply enough to bump my fist against the glass, the kiddo mirroring my movement on the other side.

But when my gaze catches Dommie's, I let those emotions loose.

I know she sees them because her smile fades, eyes going wide.

Then she shakes off her shock, smirking and holding up her hand, on which the tiny bobblehead of me with a glitter-covered beard is sitting.

She's so fucking proud of herself—and that move. I can see it in those pretty coffee-colored eyes, in her smile. So fucking beautiful and I want to go through the boards again, just to taste those tart, sass-filled, curved-up lips...and then to bend her over one of the seats and spank that lush ass of hers red.

"Later," I mouth.

Her eyes go wider.

Because she knows it's a promise.

For pleasurable payback.

For rectifying the mistakes I've made.

For...*more.*

Something else I know she sees because her mouth falls open and those pretty coffee-colored eyes widen and her cheeks turn bright red.

I want to watch that flush spread, to cover her throat, her chest, to turn her nipples into bright pink berries that call for my teeth, my tongue.

But I'm wearing a cup.

Thank *God* I'm wearing a cup.

Because when my dick starts to harden, it's confined within that hard—and incredibly uncomfortable when sporting an erection—shell, and that bolt of discomfort has me snapping out of my *promises.*

Partway, anyway.

I slip off my glove, rest my hand on the glass, something pulsing in my heart when she doesn't hesitate to lift her free palm, to place it over mine on the opposite side of the glass.

Fuck, I love this woman.

I have since that hospital waiting room.

Buzz!

Dommie jumps and I narrow my eyes, not liking they've scared her. I acknowledge the reminder from the sound crew that I need to get my ass off the ice so the arena staff can do their jobs —resurfacing the ice, final preps for puck drop—with a lift of my hand. But it still takes me a few seconds to gather the strength to pull away from this woman.

"Later," I mouth again.

She gives a shaky nod, her palm lingering on the glass for a heartbeat as I put several feet between us.

I hold that close as I skate to our bench, as I stop and speak to one of our interns who wants me to give a quote to the media.

Something I agree to, though I ask a favor in return.

I hold it close as I walk into the locker room and change my undershirt, pull on my game jersey. Hold it as Coach announces the lineup and we walk back out, skating onto the ice while music blares and lights flash and fog machines broadcast our entrance.

I hold it close as the overhead lights come back on and the anthem starts.

I hold it close, knowing that I'm not going to fuck up this time.

Because Dommie is in the stands.

And I hold it close...

Knowing that Theo's name isn't going to be on her back much longer.

Eighteen

Dommie

"Excuse me?"

I blink and tear my gaze away from the ice, looking to the left and seeing a young woman wearing a Breakers T-shirt standing in the aisle.

She has an expectant look on her face, and is holding a bag at her side.

"Hi," I say uncertainly. "Can I help you with something?"

The Zamboni is running around the rink, creating shining tracks of smoothed-out ice in its wake. Music is blaring and fans are moving up and down the aisles around the arena, going to the bathroom or getting snacks, coming back with tubs of popcorn and beers with huge, frothy heads, and garlic fries.

The woman smiles and holds out a bag.

"Oh," I say, putting my hands up, palms out. "I didn't order anything." I'm in the Club section, so there *is* a limited menu of items I can have delivered (not that I'll succumb to paying arena prices).

Her brows pull together and she glances down at the slip stapled to the top of the bag. "Are you Dommie Moreno?"

Something warm coils in my belly.

Because I have a suspicion as to what this is about—

Or rather, who's responsible for it.

"Yes," I tell her.

Her mouth curves back up as she passes it over. "Then it's for you."

"Thanks," I whisper, but she's already spinning away, already hustling back up the concrete stairs.

Leaving me with the bag.

I glance down at that slip of paper stapled just below the handle, see that—indeed—my name is scrawled there.

Feeling like I need to be surreptitious, like I'm doing something wrong, opening something private in an arena filled with twenty-thousand other people, I peer into the bag.

And feel that warmth in my belly grow.

I set the bag on the ground as I pull the jersey out, already knowing whose name is going to be on the back.

Laine.

My heart skips a beat, and I'm torn between wanting to hold it close and the urge to hurl it toward the ice.

Get it away from me! It's dangerous!

Except...no surprise, wanting to hold it close wins out.

It absolutely pummels the opposition, drapes over the fear in my belly as though it doesn't exist.

I tug off the jersey Theo gave me months ago, folding it carefully before I tuck it away in the bag. Then—

Why am I holding my breath as I pull on the jersey from Walker?

Because I'm dumb.

Because I want it.

Because—

The fabric settles around me. It's not as big as the game-worn one, but it's still loose and requires creative tucking to not be engulfed in it.

And I know I'm holding my breath because I've fully fallen

into the trap of Walker Laine, and wanting it, wanting *him,* is enough to send me scrambling for heartbreak.

"Enough," I whisper, stopping myself from getting on the roller coaster of justifying wanting Walker again.

I want him.

I'm going to take what I can get for as long as I can.

And then...I'll move on with my chin up.

Because that's what Morenos do.

Or maybe it's just what *I* do.

Either way, I'm wearing Walker's jersey when the music blares and the crowd cheers and his eyes hit mine as he steps out onto the ice for the second period.

I turn slightly, enough to show him the back.

And rotate around in time to see his mouth curve up in a sexy smile that strokes me right between the legs.

Yeah, that's what I'm going to do.

Soak in the sunlight...

And then move the fuck on.

———

It's late, and I should be in bed.

But I'm walking to the elevators anyway.

I have a pass from my sister, so no one stops me as I press the button and step into the car, riding it down to the lower level.

The doors open with a ding and I step off...

Which is where my confidence fails me.

Because...what's standing in front of me is a labyrinth of doors and hallways, with people moving hurriedly through them, everyone appearing to know exactly where they're heading. All business. Focused on their tasks at hand as they disappear into the bowels of the arena.

Meanwhile, I don't know which way to go, or where I *can* go.

Anytime I've been down here, it's with Eva or Theo or Smitty to guide my way.

They're obviously not here...and what if I get lost or stumble upon the locker room?

Or the dressing room and see...

Things that can't be unseen.

I mean, hot hockey players sudsing up in the shower wouldn't be the *worst* thing, if I'm being completely honest, but—

"Focus, Dommie," I whisper, scanning from side to side, looking for a clue as to the proper direction...or maybe to those showers—

No. Bad Dommie.

I'm looking for somewhere safe to wait for Walker without the risk of drive-by dick viewing.

"Wanna tell me what's got you smirking, Sunlight?"

I jump, jerk my gaze from the twisting corridor at the right, and whip around to see Walker leaning against a wall, arms and ankles crossed, his mouth curved into that sexy smile again. His hair is damp and messy, as though he washed it and then didn't bother to do anything beyond just shoving his hand through it.

And that's probably all he *did* do.

"Naked hockey players," I say, not about to turn down the snark just because he surprised me.

His brows come up as he pushes off the wall and starts moving toward me. "Players? As in *plural?*" The questions are laced with warning.

A warning I don't heed.

"Yup," I say, that heat in my belly growing. "I think that seeing"—I pause for a heartbeat, considering what might needle him most effectively—"*Jackson* all naked, his skin slick from the water—"

He growls as he comes closer.

"And Sam and Aiden are hot—"

"They're fucking nineteen."

"I think Aiden's twenty now," I say with a shrug.

"Aiden?" he says, stopping so close that I can feel the heat radiating off his body. "Fucking really?"

"He's legal." I shrug again. "What's it to me?"

Another growl.

But it doesn't scare me.

In fact, it only has that warmth growing, expanding from my belly down into my pussy, up toward my breasts, phantom fingers teasing me in promise—

"I think Jackson would be the best, though," I say, pretending that I'm not breathless at Walker's closeness, not wavering on my feet from those phantom fingers, from the knowledge of how well I know he can work my body. "All those muscles"—I exhale (yes, shakily) and tap my finger to my lips—"that sexy smi—*ah!*"

Suddenly, I'm hard against a big, broad chest, engulfed in spicy male, firm lips slamming down onto mine, a sleek tongue darting into my mouth—

But only for a second.

Because then I'm released and spun around, a heavy arm settling around my shoulders, and I'm being drawn forward.

Into the bowels of the arena.

Nineteen

I know she's trying to piss me off.

I know she doesn't really want Aiden or Sam or—she fucking better not—Jackson.

But I can't stop myself from reacting anyway, can't stop myself from yanking her against me, from drawing her down the hall.

Not for the dressing room—the non-public facing space where we can shower without risk of cameras...or—I send a dark glare down at the top of my woman's head—Peeping Toms.

But Dommie doesn't know that.

And the devil in me has responded to the devil in her.

She's pushing, trying to provoke a reaction?

I can do that right back.

"I bet Jackson is still showering," I mutter, drawing her down the hall. "You can get your look."

Her steps stutter and I have to keep my grip firm in order to continue moving us forward.

"And if you're lucky, Sam and Aiden will still be getting dressed—"

They had just been hitting the showers after I rushed through mine, intending to get to Dommie as quickly as possible. Not in her seat—the arena would be long empty by the time I made it out. But my plan was to meet her at her car. And if I missed her there, I would show up on the doorstep of her apartment.

Only I didn't need to do any of that.

Because I came across her just outside the elevators, looking more than a little lost.

And, apparently, ready to toss sass.

Fucking Jackson Hunter.

Really?

"I—" She digs her heels in, trying to halt our momentum, but I'm bigger and stronger and can just draw her alongside with me.

"I thought you wanted to see Jackson all slicked up," I say as we turn down the hall.

The guys' voices drift toward us, loud as always, giving shit, *also* like always.

She pulls hard against my hold, but I keep moving us forward.

"Walker," she grits out, digging her nails into my arm.

I hiss out a breath—and she immediately releases me.

"Sorry."

It's a barely audible whisper that squeezes at my heart. I halt our progress and tug her against me, her breath coming out in a rush, her hands landing on my chest. "Do that next time we're both naked, baby," I murmur, bending down and slanting my mouth over hers for a quick, hot kiss.

"Wh-what?" she stammers as I pull away.

But I'm already moving forward again, and just that quickly, her befuddlement fades. "Walker, fucking stop right now!"

But I don't stop.

I keep moving, keep dragging her behind me.

Only I'm not heading for the showers.

I veer right as the voices hit a crescendo, as her fighting against my hold peaks, and push into a room I know will be empty.

Click.

I hit the lock.

It's pitch black, and I can't see shit.

But I can hear her breathing, fast and short—or maybe that's me, my lungs working hard, my breaths coming in rapid gusts. Because I want to pin her back against the closed door, want to feel the lush softness of her body against mine. I want to strip her naked, touch and kiss every inch of her in these shadows, committing the sensation of her body to memory.

"Walker," she whispers.

I step closer, crowding into her, feeling her bump back against the door. I can barely see the outline of her profile as my eyes start to slowly adjust, but it's enough.

I lower my head, slant my mouth over hers.

She sighs, lips parting, and I take that breath into my own body, my own being.

Then she melts—breasts pressing to my chest, fingers wrapping around the tops of my shoulders, squeezing tightly enough that I feel the kiss of her nails. Her thighs against mine. Her tongue dancing out, slipping into my mouth.

I groan and release her wrist, plunging that hand into her hair, tilting her face up so I can deepen the kiss. I want to devour her, to sink into the kiss and forget everything else, to pretend that we're the only two people who exist on the planet.

My other hand goes to her hip, drawing her closer even as I push her back more firmly against the door.

"If you ever see Jackson naked," I growl, breaking away, chest heaving, my cock hard and aching as it presses against my zipper, "I'll fucking kill him."

My eyes have adjusted enough to the dark to see her mouth is swollen and glistening, that her gaze is on mine. Her cheeks will be flushed, her coffee-colored eyes dilated and hazy with pleasure and need. I can feel the hard buds of her nipples against my chest, but I want to feel the slick heat of her cunt clasping around my fingers.

"I thought you were taking me to see him," she whispers teasingly, the words glazing my lips with damp heat, calling me to kiss her again.

So, I do.

Long and deep with plenty of lips and teeth and tongue.

"Fucking *never*," I rasp, leaning into her.

A shaky breath. "Oh." A beat. "Well, what if I'd like that?"

The words send a red haze through me and my grip on her tightens, but only for a heartbeat, because then the note of humor lacing the silky question penetrates, and I know my woman is teasing me.

Oh, *now* there's going to be hell to pay.

I slip my hand from her hair and flick on the lights, blinking against the sudden brightness, but already moving, already having my punishment in mind.

I lift her up and whip us around, striding away from the door and setting her on a stack of chairs in the corner.

This puts her tits at my face level.

Fucking perfect.

But...first I need to get to them.

I reach for the hem of the jersey I bought her, start yanking it up, but when I manage to get it over her head, she surprises me by launching herself off the stack of chairs, sending them wobbling.

I stick a hand out to steady them, and then she's surprising me again.

Kneeling in front of me.

Hands coming to the button of my slacks, undoing it with a flick of her fingers.

"Sunlight," I rasp in warning, my heart suddenly in my throat.

But she's grabbing the tag of my zipper, drawing it down.

"Dommie," I whisper.

She ignores me as she slips a hand into my underwear, pulls out my cock.

"*This* dick," she groans.

And then *I'm* the one who's groaning as she leans in, lips parting, allowing the head of my cock to come to her mouth.

But she doesn't take me inside.

She blows lightly, sending a violent shiver through me.

Then her tongue darts out, slipping into the slit at the crown of my dick, and I curse under my breath.

A glance up at me, eyes dancing with feminine power, and I expect her to draw this out, to keep teasing me.

Instead, she surprises me again.

Always fucking surprising me.

Letting me back into her life.

Making it so I can never predict what she's going to say, going to do—

In this case, it's with very pleasurable results.

Those lips part, and she takes me deep into her mouth.

TWENTY

DOMMIE

I fucking *love* giving blow jobs.

The power that I feel.

The strength in a simple flick of my tongue, in the positioning of my hand, in the tightness of my grip.

I can bring this man to his knees.

Even though *I'm* currently the one who's kneeling.

He growls low in his throat and I shiver, but I don't slow down, don't stop taking him deep, gripping him tight. His cock is so big and hard that it strains the corners of my mouth, making them ache and sting, but I don't slow down or stop now either.

Because it's a good pain, a good ache—one that has my already wet pussy getting even wetter.

I moan as the hard length of him hits the back of my throat, pumping my hand in time to the strokes of my tongue, swallowing him deep enough to make my eyes water, to have me struggling to not cough, to not gag.

But I don't stop.

Because even though tears are clinging to my eyelashes, I fucking *love* doing this to Walker.

Sweat gleams on his forehead.

His hair is a mess from that post-game shower lack of styling and me running my fingers through it.

His beard is scruffy and dark and thick, and I can almost feel the scrape of it against my skin, lightly abrading as he makes his way down to my pussy.

I'm the one who's in charge in this moment.

And yet, he sends me close to the edge with just his eyes.

How they've locked with mine, absolutely scorching, pinning me in place, making my pulse skitter and my heart launch itself against my rib cage.

But I don't stop sucking him deep.

I don't stop stroking and licking and—

"Fuck!"

I can't really smile with his dick in my mouth, but the satisfaction I get from the way he growls out that curse has the corners of my lips turning up, even as I keep blowing him—just now with the addition of me gently massaging his balls.

There's salt on my tongue, and I know he's close.

So, I squeeze a little tighter, suck him a little deeper, stroke a little faster, massage just the tiniest bit more firmly.

"Dommie," he rasps in warning.

I know he's close, even without him giving me that warning, without his fingers gripping my hair, trying to tug me off.

I know that he's close and I'm *not fucking stopping*.

"*Fuck,*" he growls as the first jets of his cum hit the back of my throat. "Fuck, baby, *fuck!*"

More cum in my mouth, filling it so full that I struggle to keep up as I swallow, the tart saltiness coating my tongue.

"Christ," he mutters a few moments later as I stop stroking and pull carefully back, licking my lips. A flash of guilt across that handsome face. "I wasn't—" A shake of his head. "Baby, I wasn't trying to—"

"I know." I touch my fingers to his jaw when he pulls me to my feet, feeling the bristles of his beard on my skin. "I *wanted* to."

I mean, I didn't plan it.

And it's probably stupid as shit to be here like this with Walker.

He works here.

I'm opening a storefront several levels above.

I—

He touches my cheek. "I was just hoping to catch you at your car. Not—" His eyes flick down and he reaches down, adjusts himself, the *ziiip* of his slacks loud in the quiet office. "Not that."

I worry my bottom lip, guilt slicing through me. "You didn't like it? I know it was dumb to do that here—"

He presses his forehead to mine. "It's the best fucking blow job I've ever had."

I can hear the sincerity in his words, in the flex of his fingers as he drops his hands to my waist. "Oh," I whisper.

"And I'm going to reciprocate," he murmurs silkily, one hand sliding to my ass, yanking me flush against him. "Just not where Jackson or Sam or Aiden can stumble onto us."

Guilt swirls in my belly. "I didn't think," I whisper. "I'm sorry—"

"I started it." Another tug, drawing me even closer. "And don't you fucking apologize"—he slants a heated look in my direction—"if you hadn't been the one on your knees, I would have been."

Desire blooming between my thighs.

"It's just likely that"—loud voices in the hall have both of our gazes turning toward the door—"our moment of privacy has passed."

"Oh." I wince. "Right."

Fingers on my cheek. "Don't worry," he says lightly.

"You work here," I whisper, guilt churning in my belly. "I could have gotten you in trouble."

"Sunlight." His fingers go to my jaw, tilt my face up. "If you think this is the only time someone has gotten busy in this arena, then you clearly don't understand hockey players."

My brows pull together. "Ew," I mutter.

"I picked this closet for a reason"—he grins—"Luc and Lexi got caught in here not that long ago."

My brows shoot up. "The GM?"

He nods. "Don't forget that half the guys are married to women who work for the team."

That was slightly less vomit-inducing than Walker picking this closet because he was down here with puck bunnies who were...

Something *more* than me.

That slender blonde woman flashes through my mind again.

His fingers tighten on my jaw and he bends a little to meet my eyes. "What just went through your mind?"

"Nothing," I say, tugging at the hem of the jersey, straightening it before I step back, spotting my purse and the bag with Theo's jersey on the industrial carpet.

"Bullshit."

Crap.

I grit my teeth and look back, forcing my trademark fake smile. The one I plaster on when my mom is being her horrible self, when her carefully constructed barbs slice deep. I reach for my bags, hanging them off my wrists as I rotate back to face him. "Just my bags. See?" I lift my arms.

His eyes narrow, and I know he's not going to let this go.

So, I engage invasive maneuvers.

"How many women have you brought to this closet?"

Clarity in deep brown eyes.

He comes closer, holding my stare. "One."

My lungs go tight.

Because there's no doubt that he's telling me the truth.

"Oh," I whisper.

"Anything else running through that big, juicy brain of yours?"

So, *so* many things. All of which I can't tell him, can't afford to even think about. Which is why I just shake my head and say, "No."

He lightly touches his fingertips to my cheek, crouches again so our gazes are aligned, staring deep into my eyes for a long moment.

Then his expression softens, his palm cups my jaw, and he says, "Okay, then, baby. Let's go home."

Twenty-One

Walker

The buzzing comes what feels like two minutes after I closed my eyes, and I stifle a groan as I slam into consciousness far too fucking early.

The bed shifts and the buzzing ceases, and I hear Dommie sigh softly.

Then her fingers wrap around my wrist and she lifts my arm off her belly.

Or tries to, anyway.

Because I roll with her, drawing her back against my chest. "Mmm," I murmur, brushing my lips over the top of her ear. "Morning, baby."

She melts against me, fingers tightening on my wrists, back arching, ass pressing against my pelvis.

Last night, we came back to my house, and I made good on my promise to return the favor.

She came—twice—and then I came again, and then we both passed out.

Now, morning has come far too soon.

I kiss the side of her neck, inhaling the sweetness of her scent, not wanting to move.

"I really do have to get up," she murmurs, but her body is still heavy against mine, and I know that I can coax her to stay a little longer, to stretch out this moment, to maybe even be late into the bakery.

But we're at my house.

Which means she's not around the corner from the bakery.

The drive is longer, and she needs to leave earlier if she's going to make it to work on time.

She can't afford any sexy interludes delaying her today.

I exhale and release her. "I'll start the shower," I say, slipping from beneath the blankets. "Then I'll make coffee. Are you hungry?" I ask, turning for the bathroom. "I can make you something." I flick on the lights, hating the way they stab at my eyes, hating that Dommie has to be up at the asscrack of dawn to go to work when she should be sleeping in, should be pampered and protected and—

I frown as I come out of the bathroom, finding her body all but frozen in bed.

Not asleep.

I can see those pretty coffee-colored eyes from the open bathroom door, can read the panic in those depths as I walk back over to her.

"Baby?"

She doesn't move.

"*Baby.*"

A blink, and then her lids slide closed for a long moment.

I touch her shoulder.

Her eyes flash open, and she sits up so quickly that we almost crack skulls. I jerk back, feeling the rush of air between our heads, the near miss making my heart skip a beat. "Sunlight," I say quietly, grabbing the tops of her arms and steadying her. "Careful, baby."

"I'm sorry," she whispers, hand lifting between us. Her fingers brush my forehead. "I'm just...sorry," she says, so softly that I can barely hear it.

I frown, shifting us so that she's sitting in my lap. "What's the matter?"

Silence then, "Nothing's the matter. It's just early and I'm out of it."

This is true.

It's early as shit, and I'm sure she's tired after last night.

But that's not what's wrong.

"Lies in a trash can," I blurt.

Another blink, but this one isn't long, and it's not accompanied by a side of almost braining me. "What did you say?"

"Lies—" I draw her closer. "In a—" Kiss the top of her head. "Trash can."

More silence.

Then, "I don't know what you're talking about."

"I'm talking about you trying to bullshit me again. Put those lies right in the trash can and tell me what's got you tweaked. Is it sleeping here? Picking up where we broke off? Too much time together?" I cup her jaw.

"It's—" Her teeth press into her bottom lip and then she exhales. "It's all just moving kind of fast and...I'm tired, Walker." She scoots off my lap. "That's really it. You've got to give me a few minutes for my brain to start working, okay?"

She meets my eyes then glances away.

That's part of it, maybe even a lot of it.

It *is* the butt crack of dawn.

We had a late night.

She has to work.

So...I give her that.

"Okay, baby," I murmur, not missing that her body has gone stiff, and that with my words, it relaxes. "But also know that I'm not going anywhere."

Those shoulders rise again, hunching. "Right," she whispers.

It's early.

I'm exhausted.

But I don't miss the disbelief in her eyes, her frame, her tone.

I don't like it—not at fucking all—but this isn't the right time, and as much as I hate it and want to pretend that the shit didn't happen, I hurt her. I got her to trust me and then pushed her away and she doesn't believe me.

That's on me.

Just like it's on me to be patient until she gets it.

Until she understands what I knew from the first time I pulled her close in the emergency department's waiting room.

That's she's mine.

Until goddamned *reasons* got in the way.

Guilt and fury rage through me and I bite back a curse, push off the mattress, and extend a hand, holding my breath until her palm is resting against mine.

"Shower, Sunlight," I say gently. "And I'll make you breakfast."

That little startle again, but she shakes it off, slipping her hand from mine. "Okay," she whispers. "Thanks."

I cup her jaw, press my lips to her forehead.

Then I'm walking out of the bedroom.

And making my woman banana nut pancakes.

Because they're her favorite.

Something I learned how to make when I found out she loves them.

Because the look she gives me when she comes down from the bedroom, her skin pink from the heat of the shower, and she sees those damned pancakes on the plate, slays me.

Surprise.

Pleasure.

Softness.

I'll do anything for this woman.

Anything.

Including letting her walk out the door, get in the car I followed over from the arena the night before, and drive away.

———

I'm sitting in my office, reviewing tape, when there's a knock at my front door.

My eyes flick to the clock in the upper right of my computer screen, see that it's too early for Dommie to be done with work—

And I highly doubt she'll drive back to my place.

I still have a shit-ton of work to do there.

So, I've been planning on showing up at her apartment again —or maybe, better yet, just meeting at the bakery so she can't escape, muahaha—

Knock. Knock. Knock.

"Right," I mutter, closing my laptop and getting up to go answer the door. It's certainly not Dommie, so likely it's one of my teammates here to torture me.

Which means that even if I ignore them, they won't go away.

So...might as well get this shit over with.

Deal with those assholes—okay, *friends*—and their forced socialization—okay, *hanging out*, like friends do—and get back to the tape, and then get back to Dommie.

There.

Plan made.

Great.

Break.

I walk out into the hall and move toward the front door, frowning when I see more than one shadow through the frosted glass.

Teammates then. *Plural.*

Christ.

I curse under my breath, accept that I'm the loser in the who's gonna host the Breakers latest gaming session, say a mental goodbye to my beer and snacks, and reach for the knob.

Pull open the door.

And I'm slapped in the fucking face with...

Reasons.

Twenty-Two

I expected him to show up at the bakery.

When he didn't, I expected him to be waiting for me at my apartment—or maybe *inside* my apartment, somehow commandeering a key or acquiring those secret agent skills he teased me about having a few days ago, or...

I just expected him, okay?

I shouldn't have.

But...stupidity and hope and that tiny piece inside me that was shriveled and brown, but somehow still alive had thought—

"It doesn't matter," I whisper, stirring the veggies I cut up that will make the bulk of my simple stew. Along with some leftover beef, I've added potatoes, carrots, celery, onions, and peas. Warm, hearty, and paired with the sourdough currently baking in the oven—made easy thanks to my starter, Bob—it's going to be perfect for dinner on a cold, wintery night.

My dinner for one.

I wrinkle my nose as I turn for the oven, tugging open the door and peeking at my loaf.

The crust is almost there.

I want the inside as fluffy as a cloud, and the outside layer a deep brown and with enough substance that my jaw gets tired from chewing.

That's a sourdough.

Since I have a few minutes left—the stew needs thickening and that crust needs to get chewier, I take the opportunity to pop down the hall and run a bath.

Food.

Bubbles.

A dash of homework—because that's a surefire way to put me to sleep, especially when it's putting the finishing touches on my business plan for Professor Johnson, *er*, Todd's class.

Tomorrow's my day off.

Which is really just a day for me to cram in all of my errands and adult tasks.

Grocery shopping, paying bills, meal prep, homework, scrubbing my toilet.

All the fun, grown-up responsibilities.

I add a capful of bubbles. They're pricey, but I love the scent and so I use them on very special occasions.

Like soaking until I'm pruney so I can forget about a certain broody hockey player.

Shaking my head, I watch the bubbles start to form and exhale.

Then I go back to the kitchen. And I eat my stew and bread.

Later, my jaw is tired. My belly is full.

My skin is pruney, and my lids are heavy as hell, but my business plan is done, and I've sorted out meals for the week and my grocery list, and consumed far too many episodes of a reality TV show I'm addicted to. And by *consumed*, I mean it's playing in the background while I do all of the other life tasks I've tackled because actually watching it without anything to partially distract me makes me want to gouge my eyes out.

Does that make sense?

No.

But I'm still addicted anyway.

Probably why I'm reaching for the remote, intending to hit the button to skip the credits and dive into the next episode, all while scrolling through my business plan one last time and only half paying attention to the TV when there's a knock at the door.

It's barely eight, but I've been in my pajamas for hours now.

No bra beneath my tank top and silky button-down and lounge pants. I am wearing my favorite brand of undies (these ones are boy cut and patterned with drunken unicorns), but I'm still in no position to answer the door.

Knock. Knock. Knock.

I lift up my phone, try to load the doorbell camera, but as is often the case with this apartment building, the fucking internet sucks.

Thick walls or old service, I don't know.

I just can't load the feed.

And so I have a decision to make.

Ignore it—

Knock! Knock! Knock!

Or pretend like I'm not home.

But even as I consider that, whoever's on my fucking porch knocks again.

Groaning, and chucking my phone with the useless camera feed to the side, I move to the front door and yank it open—

I would be lying if I said that I wasn't hoping it was Walker.

Running late, but still coming to see me.

Sticking around as promised.

But it's not Walker on the other side of the door.

Instead, it's—

"Professor Johnson?" I ask incredulously.

His gaze does a long, slow trail down my body, and in no way is it sexy. In no way does it make me feel anything but skeevy, especially as he drags it back up just as slowly until his eyes meet mine. "Todd, remember?" he tells me.

I shudder, fingers clenching on the door, vowing to never open it without knowing who's on the other side again.

Because I don't like the look in his eyes.

I don't like the way he's staring at me.

I don't like...

How he steps closer, pushing me back into my apartment. Not physically, but spatially, forcing me to take several paces away from him if I don't want our bodies to touch.

And I don't.

Because...skeevy.

And that's how I find myself with my lower back pressed to the edge of the small table I keep in the hall. I dump my mail and purse and keys there, and below is my shoe rack. Next to it, I have a coat tree, loaded up with everything from hoodies to my heavy winter jacket.

None of those things help me, though, as Professor Johnson totters closer.

His eyes are glassy and I can smell the alcohol on his breath.

"Did you drive here?" I ask.

His mouth curves up into a smile, and he's objectively hand-some, that twitch of his lips movie-star worthy—albeit *still* skeevy. "I'm taking you to dinner," he announces.

I frown, look down at my pajamas, and then back up at him. "No," I say. "I'm getting ready for bed."

"It's still early," he says, swinging out an arm.

It knocks into my coatrack, sending the metal contraption crashing to the floor.

Thank God I'm on the ground floor.

No neighbors to piss off.

"Get your coat," he orders, bending unsteadily toward my rack, yanking my heavy jacket off the hook, and straightening. "Here," he says, thrusting it at me.

The material hitting my chest snaps me out of my shock—or maybe it's the realization that I don't mind orders from Walker, but hearing them from Professor Johnson pisses me off—and I grab my coat from him, toss it to the side. It skids across the floor, but I don't give a fuck. "You need to go," I tell him as I walk toward the door, my fingers clenching on the heavy wooden and metal panel. "Right now, Professor Johnson. This is really inappropriate and—"

Suddenly, he's in my face, moving far too quickly, getting far too close. "Let's go," he slurs.

Whiskey.

It's whiskey on his breath.

Which would have been enough for me to not get into the car with him, but adding in the creepiness, the utter fucking gall of showing up here without my permission, leapfrogging over copious boundaries, and I'll be getting into his car over my dead body.

"Come on," he says, fingers wrapping around my wrist.

I bat at his hand, but he takes me by surprise again, yanking me forward in a movement I don't anticipate.

And then I'm outside my apartment, the cold cutting through the thin material of my clothes, razor blades slicing along my skin.

My socks are instantly wet, and I gasp, struggling against his hold.

Which just tightens as he continues to draw me forward.

"Professor Johnson," I say, my lungs struggling to form the words in the frosty air.

His head whips back around. "*Todd,*" he snaps, expression even icier than the snow piled along the edges of the sidewalk.

My mouth falls open, but I get it together, lifting my chin. "Let me go."

He leans closer, that whiskey breath in my nose again. "*Todd,*" he growls.

"Let me go, *Todd,*" I snap.

His mouth starts to form a word, and I can already see that it's not *Sure* or *Okay, Dommie.*

It's *no.*

But he doesn't get it out because suddenly my wrist is torn from his fingers, and I'm tucked behind a big, warm, *solid* body.

Chocolate brown eyes meet mine as Walker looks back over his shoulder.

"In the house, Sunlight," he says gently. *Carefully.*

But I don't miss that there's murder in his expression.

Twenty-Three

Walker

That fucker has his hands on her.

Or *had* them because now *Todd* is sprawled out on the fucking ground, staring up at me with glazed eyes. Christ.

I saw his car in the lot when I pulled in.

And instantly knew that I fucked around in my head about *reasons* for too goddamned long.

One knock on my door and I wanted to fucking run again, to call this off, to keep Dommie safely out of the mess that's my life.

I actually convinced myself of that...after I got rid of *reasons*.

But as the afternoon wore on and the sun set and I sat in my empty fucking house, I knew that I was making a mistake.

The biggest fucking mistake of my life.

Because I already did this once—pushed Dommie away—and I was miserable. The thought of doing it again, after knowing how fucking perfect she is, after knowing what it's like to *not* have her, is even worse.

And now, I'm here at her apartment complex, and I'm seeing this motherfucker with his hands on her, and—

I reach down and grab *Todd* by the collar of his shirt, hauling him toward me.

Lifting my other fist, intending to plow it into the fucker's face.

"Don't," Dommie says, grabbing onto my arm. "He's not worth you destroying your career over."

I squeeze my hand, manage to stop glaring at the asshole whose face has pulled into a sneer, and glance over at Dommie. "He touched you," I growl.

Something changes in her face, but she doesn't drop her hand, doesn't try to tug mine from the fucker's throat. She just moves a little closer, her front pressing to the side of my arm, her hand sliding up to rest on my shoulder. "I'm okay," she whispers.

He'd yanked her forward like a goddamned rag doll.

And her face—

Fuck, she'd been terrified.

My fingers tighten.

The fucker chokes.

Just not hard enough.

Then I feel it.

Dommie shivering.

"Christ," I mutter, loosening my grip, just slightly, because the fucker is turning blue. With my other hand, I reach into the pocket of my pants and tug out my phone, dialing a number for the second time today.

Detective McKay picks up on the second ring. "Don't have any updates for you yet—"

"Listen," I say, interrupting him, well aware that my voice is near guttural, that my temper is razor thin, that Dommie is fucking cold. "My woman was just assaulted at her apartment complex."

"Where?" John says, pivoting in a second, as he's wont to do.

"What?" *Todd* says, glassy eyes widening. "She wanted to go to dinner with me and—*argh!*"

I tighten my fingers again, cutting off the flow of bullshit.

I give the address, and add, "He's drunk and can barely stand up." Never mind that might be partly to do with my hand around his throat that's slowly preventing fresh air from entering his body. I can smell the whiskey from here. My eyes flick to the guest spot in front of Dommie's place.

The one I couldn't park in.

Because this asshole's car is in it, the lights on, the driver's side door wide fucking open.

Goddamned idiot.

Who opens his mouth and begins to protest in a loud, slurred voice, "I'm not drunk. I'm just taking her to dinner—"

I shake him.

Detective McKay curses under his breath. "I'm not far from that complex," he mutters after he's turned my ears blue—and that's saying something, considering that I grew up in locker rooms. "Get yourself and your woman safe. I'll be there in five."

He clicks off.

Todd glares at me, his glassy eyes barely visible beneath half-closed lids.

Dommie shivers.

And...

My fingers tighten.

———

She still doesn't have any fucking shoes on.

Or a jacket.

I want to tear open the front door, storm down the walk, and yank open the back of the police cruiser where *Todd* is currently taking up residence and choke him all over again.

For real this time.

Until those glassy eyes slide closed, and the last bit of life leaves his body.

"I guess I don't need this," Dommie murmurs, and I turn,

seeing her lift her open laptop from the couch, watching as she taps on the keyboard and closes the screen.

"Don't need what?" I rasp as I bend to retrieve her coat from the floor and walk across the room, wrapping it around her shoulders. She's still shivering, even though it's warm in the apartment, and I nudge her back onto the couch, lifting each foot in turn in order to tug off her wet socks. They land with soft *flops* on the hardwood.

"My business plan," she says, nibbling at the corner of her mouth when I cup one foot between my hands and rub gently, using friction to warm it.

"Why won't you need your business plan?" I ask, repeating the same process with the other foot.

"Because I can't go back to Professor Johnson's class," she whispers.

Rage coils down my spine and I have to force myself to keep my hold gentle. "I don't think Professor Johnson is going to be back in class, baby."

Because Detective McKay took one look at the asshole, muttered to me that this wasn't *Todd's* first time being arrested for driving under the influence *and* trespassing.

Her nostrils flare on her inhale. "Oh," she whispers. "Right."

But I see she doesn't completely believe me.

And look, I get it.

Powerful men get off all the time.

I know this from my own experience. My dad—a powerful man in his own right—never paid a dollar of child support until he was forced to after a years' long legal battle with my mom. Instead, he used me as a pawn while my mother struggled to put food in our fridge and skates on my feet.

So yeah, I know that powerful men assault people, incite violence, use and abuse and walk free *all* the fucking time.

But my Dommie isn't going to deal with that shit.

I lean in, cup her jaw for a second, and then reach beyond her for the blanket, tugging it down and wrapping it around her.

"Regardless, I'll go with you to the next class, just to make sure, okay?"

Her eyes widen, and she starts to shake her head. "That's okay. I'm fine—"

But I'm back in front of her, hands resting on her knees, my gaze holding hers.

"I'm *going* with you."

Her lips press flat and her eyes slide away from mine for a long moment before they drift back. I see the resignation in the coffee-colored depths. "You're not going to let this go, are you?" she asks softly.

"I'm here," I say. "I told you this morning that I'm here and I'm going to stay *here*."

Despite all the *reasons* knocking on my goddamned door.

Her eyes stay on mine and she studies me for several long moments before she nods. "You're here to stay."

Those words are everything that I want to hear.

And yet...they don't ring true.

Maybe it's something in her tone. Maybe it's something in the way her eyes change, emotions gathering at the edges of her expression.

Maybe it's just because it's been a shit day and I spent half of it convincing myself of that same truth—that I'm here, that I have staying power—so I feel like a fucking asshole.

But I don't have a chance to address any of that.

Because Detective McKay knocks on the door.

I let him in, and turn back to Dommie, hating the dark circles beneath her eyes, the chaos on the coffee table that tells of a pleasant night in that was interrupted.

That I missed out on because I was up my own ass.

Guilt churns.

Regret burns.

And then I have to sit beside my woman as she gives her statement about the man who assaulted her.

Twenty-Four

"Did you hear about Professor Johnson getting arrested?"

"Yes!" a girl behind me says. "I heard he got a DUI."

"*I* heard he assaulted a student," Kurt says on a sigh from a few desks over.

"Really?" the girl says.

"Yup." Kurt grins. "Damn, I love a bad boy. Why couldn't *I* be the student he assaulted?"

"Seriously," Hayley says, fanning herself. "He can be his bad boy self with me *any* time he wants." A beat. "No assault necessary."

I flick my stare to the side, lifting my brows at Walker—who, as promised—has crammed his big body into the desk next to mine.

He scowls, but his hand reaches beneath the folded-out surface he pulled from the armrest of the desk he's sitting in, and he squeezes my knee gently.

But he doesn't speak.

Or rather, he doesn't get the chance to.

Because another teacher walks into the room.

She's tall and beautiful and is wearing a no-nonsense expression as she plugs in her laptop, sending a slide projecting onto the whiteboard. "Let's get it over with," she says into the curious silence that's fallen. "Professor Johnson won't be returning to this class." Whispers start up. "Or the university." They get louder. "Now"—her voice increases in volume until she's practically yelling over the talking that's begun—"I'm Professor Bernard, and let's talk about your business plans that are due Thursday."

There's a collective groan, but that reminder proves to be effective in focusing us, and pretty soon I'm lost in a lecture that's significantly more comprehensive and entertaining than anything Professor Johnson had given.

I barely realize it's been a full hour, not snapping out of my intrigued fog until she dismisses us.

There's a moment of silence, everyone clearly as enthralled as I had been, before we all start moving, packing up our stuff and filing out of the classroom.

"Ms. Moreno—"

I freeze on the stairs, Walker's big hand tensing where it's resting on my back.

I turn around, the stream of students moving around me, and around Walker, because he's right behind me.

"Do you have a moment?" Professor Bernard's eyes flick over my shoulder, no doubt taking in Walker's sturdy and—I flick a gaze up—*scowling* expression.

I tear my gaze from his and grind my back teeth together, hating the trepidation building in my stomach. "Yes," I say despite that, starting to move down the stairs.

I feel Walker move with me and glance up again. "It's okay."

Chocolate brown eyes on mine, that scowl deepening as he studies me for a beat. Then his big chest lifts and falls on a breath. "I'll be right outside the door," he says, reading rightfully that he's not going to win this one. "The *open* door," he adds quietly.

I squeeze his hand, knowing his protective instincts have been piqued. He stayed with me all day yesterday, came to the bakery this morning, and even though he has practice in a few hours, he's here. With me. Sitting through my classes. *All* day. "Thanks, honey," I say softly.

His face gentles, the scowl poofing away, and he nods shortly before sliding my backpack from my shoulders and carrying it clenched in one hand as he starts walking up the stairs.

"Bodyguard?" Professor Bernard says softly.

"Something like that," I say back.

Silence falls.

Then she shakes her head. "I talk for a living," she murmurs. "But I find myself at a loss for words." A sigh. "I'm sorry he did that to you."

I shiver, feeling the tight grip on my wrist, the cold on my feet, the sinking sensation that came from knowing I couldn't muscle my way out of his hold gripping me again. I knew I wouldn't be able to stop him from dragging me toward his car, knew that...bad shit was going to happen.

Things I didn't want—

"I'm sorry," Professor Bernard whispers and my eyes snap open. "If you would like to drop this class, I'll help you make that happen. Otherwise, please let me know if you need a little extra time on Thursday's assignment—"

"It's done already," I blurt.

Her expression changes. Guilt laced with amusement now. "Why did I figure that would be the case with our star student?"

And that's when I remember.

She'd been at the networking dinner last week.

Never too close to Professor Johnson, but on the periphery of the conversation.

Had he done something to—?

I clamp my lips together before I take this conversation too far.

I don't know this woman, and nothing bad really happened to me. It was scary and unnerving and I didn't like it.

But it was also a twenty-foot march out on a cold sidewalk.

And...a man forcing his way into my house.

I shudder and push the last thought out of my head. "Thank you for the offer," I say, hastily erecting some distance between us, between the fear in my belly and the sadness in this woman's eyes that spoke of bad shit, of things she didn't want. "But I'm good," I add. "Really, I am."

A blip of silence, then Professor Bernard is nodding, her smile steady, albeit a bit frayed at the edges. "I'm glad," she says. "Let me know if that changes, and I look forward to seeing your business plan."

I smile and nod hastily, turning for the stairs, starting up them.

But I pause on the third one, rotate back, seeing that she's unplugged her computer and is shoving it into her bag.

"Professor Bernard?"

She glances up. "Yes, Dominique?"

For once, I don't hate my name as it dances off her tongue. The hard letter sounds softened by the gentleness of her voice.

It's beautiful, and thus, takes me a second to realize I'm standing on that third step, staring at her.

Not saying anything.

Ugh.

My cheeks heat, but I straighten my shoulders and press on anyway.

It's what Morenos do.

Or...it's what Moreno kids do.

"I really enjoyed your lecture today," I say. "And I'm looking forward to Thursday's."

There's more silence—this time stunned rather than uncomfortable or curious.

Then she zips up her backpack and lifts it, threading an arm through both straps. "Thank you," she says, wrapping a scarf around her neck.

Right.

I'm making this weird.

I should go.

So, I bob a nod and turn around, starting up the stairs again.

"Dominique?"

I freeze, rotate back toward her.

Professor Bernard is smiling, and there's not a hint of sadness, of bad shit, or unwanted things in it. "Thursday's is even better," she says, smile widening into a grin.

I grin back.

Nod again.

"I can't wait."

And then I hustle up the rest of the stairs, through the door that Walker has—indeed—propped open, and step into my big, broody hockey player's arms.

I kiss him quickly before taking his free hand and drawing us back toward our cars.

Another kiss before he gets in his.

He has practice to get to.

I have another class to attend.

And *then* I have a business plan to proofread one last time.

Twenty-Five

Walker

"Glitter!" Smitty booms as I stride into the locker room, my messenger bag over one shoulder.

He's sporting a giant grin that's unfortunately not hidden by his huge beard visible.

Asshole.

I narrow my eyes at him, but don't engage.

It's like chumming the water when sharks are nearby.

He'll circle and wait...then launch toward the surface in a burst of shocking speed.

Shocking because *I'll* be the prey.

I shove my bag onto the shelf overhead, start checking my gear, making sure everything looks right. Not that the equipment guys don't do a fucking awesome job—packing up all of our gear, including extras like spare sticks and skate blades and all manner of tape, along with all of our jerseys, base layers, and more—but this is one of those pregame rituals I always do.

Like shooting over the net.

Shoulder pads. Check. Shinguards—one, two. Check. Skates

and elbow pads and gloves—two of each. Check. Hockey pants. Jersey. A pair of socks. My jock. All there.

And when I turn back around, fucking Smitty is too.

Christ.

I grit my teeth, go for neutral. "What's up?" I ask.

His head ticks to the side, eyes narrowing. "I've heard a rumor," he drawls, tapping a finger to his stupid grin. "About a certain Moreno."

My teeth grind so tightly together that pain shoots through my jaw, but I don't bite, just start peeling off my jacket, hanging it on one of the hooks embedded into the wall.

We're playing in Buffalo today, and the away locker rooms in most arenas are not designed for comfort.

We'll have to tough it out without any perks like our gaming room and hot and cold baths, and our fully-stocked kitchen.

Though—thank you, hockey gods—Claire is still here.

Assisting the team.

Anticipating anything any of the guys might need, and having it available even before we realize we *do* need it.

Case in point?

Right at this moment she's walking through the door, wheeling a cooler behind her that I know is filled with all of our favorite drinks.

There's also a table set up and shoved against the wall, baskets of pregame snacks at the ready.

Mostly protein bars for sustained energy and fortified liquids for that quick shot of power, something that'll hit fast and hard, but won't last the whole game.

And there's also...

A hot dog.

Because that's what Aiden wants as his pregame meal.

A fucking gas station hot dog, eaten all of twenty minutes before puck drop. The thought has me gagging—because first of all, hot dogs are barely edible, but getting them from a random gas station and then having them sit out and get cold is even worse.

Regardless—no matter the city, no matter the time of the game—Claire always manages to have one waiting for him.

And roasted but unsalted almonds for Marcel.

And a chocolate muffin for Raph. Lemon-lime Gatorade for me.

A table of favorites—new and old—of items to assuage superstitions, of a variety of pregame fuels. Something for everyone. We all know it. We all appreciate it.

But Jackson is the only one who's locked eyes on her.

Whose expression is burning with need.

Whose whole world stops when Claire walks through the door.

"A rumor about a certain Moreno who was shooting daggers through her eyes at you last time we were all together and—"

I throw a roll of tape Smitty, maybe a little harder than necessary, but it serves to cut off his fishing mission and when I tilt my head to the side—toward Claire and Jackson—it also serves to refocus that gossip-minded brain on someone who's *not* me.

On Jackson.

And Claire.

His brows are arched high when he looks back at me, and the twinkle in his eyes has me settling.

The focus is off me.

For the moment, anyway.

I exhale silently as Smitty booms, "Something caught your eye, Jackson?"

My scowly teammate whips his head away from where Claire is setting up the cooler, and narrows his eyes.

At Smitty.

At me.

I put my hands up in surrender, but he sees right through my bullshit, and his expression promises payback.

"Thanks for the drinks, Clairey girl!" Smitty calls, voice ringing around the room.

Her cheeks go bright pink, shoulders hunching, but she lifts her head, plasters on a smile, and nods once. "You're welcome," she says. "Let me know if you need anything else." She starts for the door.

"How was your date?"

Her pace picks up.

Her cheeks go brighter.

"It was fine, Smitty," she says, and there's a line of firmness that I wouldn't dare dance over.

Smitty, though, has no such compunction.

He cha-chas right on by.

"Fine doesn't exactly scream a good date," Smitty says, loudly as always.

Those shoulders hitch higher. "Bye, Smitty."

"Did he do something?"

The air in the locker room tenses, Jackson taking a leap the rest of us were several paces behind in making.

"Did he *hurt* you?" Jackson asks, not in Smitty-volume, but clearly enough to be heard throughout the entire room, especially with the rest of us falling quiet, putting pieces together that we really didn't like.

Had the asshole hurt our Claire?

Because if he had, we are all about to get arrested.

I can see the headline now, *Breakers Players Pummel Asshole Who Deserved It*.

Or...maybe not.

"It's not like that," she says, moving to the door even more quickly. "I have other things—"

Jackson stands, moves over to her, takes her arm. "Did. He. *Hurt.* You?"

And I watch as quiet, sweet Claire displays even more steel.

Her chin goes up.

Her eyes narrow.

She yanks her arm from Jackson's hold, shoves his chest hard. "Don't you fucking touch me." He drops his hand to his side, and if his expression had promised me retribution earlier, Claire's now promises murder. "He stood me up, okay?" She takes a step back. "Only he *didn't*. Not really, anyway. Because I watched in the mirror behind the bar as he walked through the restaurant door, took one look at me, and turned right around again and strolled on out." Her shoulders rise and fall on a breath. "So, yeah, he hurt me, just not how you think."

Now the room goes quiet, awkward.

But I don't have the chance to fix that.

Because Claire's already gone.

And Jackson has followed her.

———

I drop my bag onto the bed and dig out my charging cable, plugging it into the wall, setting my phone to charge before I yank out some sweats, a tee, and turn on the TV, trying to calm my mind.

The game went well—we won, and even though it was a grind, we did some good things, got those two points. Is there shit we need to tighten up, to improve on, other things we need to change? Abso-fucking-lutely. There always is.

But...we're looking pretty fucking good.

We did a quick post-game cooldown—without any of the perks of our home arena—and then hopped on a plane, heading to the next city.

One more game tomorrow and then I'll be home.

Be with Dommie.

Things are going better than I can hope.

She's not freezing me out. We've been spending time together. She's come to another game, gone out to dinner with me—we kept the reservation this time—and she even met me at my place before I left for this road trip with a bag full of warm apple cinnamon muffins.

I've had a couple of weeks of her in my life, a couple of weeks that have been fucking great.

I just...

She's holding back.

And I can't say I blame her.

Twenty-Six

Buzz-buzz.
  Buzz-buzz.
  Buzz-buzz.

My brows drag together and I lift an arm that feels way too heavy to rub the sleep from my eyes, taking a long moment to clue into the fact that my phone vibrating on my nightstand isn't actually my alarm, but my phone ringing.

No. It's my phone chiming with a video call.

From Walker.

"What the hell?" I mutter, worry in my belly as I reach for it, seeing the clock in the upper left saying it's a minute before my alarm is supposed to go off.

I watched the game last night, knew he and the team (and my sister) were supposed to leave shortly after the final buzzer and travel to Boston for another away game tomorrow.

Had something gone wrong?

I swipe at the screen. "Hello? Walker?"

"Sunlight."

The relaxed, sleepy rumble has the rough edges inside

smoothing out, the anxiety that had ramped in one short moment of wakefulness settle.

"Walker," I say again. "Is everything okay?" I ask, needing to be certain, needing to hear it from him even though part of me knows that it is by the way he said *Sunlight*.

"Yeah, baby," he murmurs. "I just wanted to hear your voice before you left for work."

"I—" I push up in bed, gathering the covers against my chest, my heart thudding hard against my ribs. That was sweet, just like this man has been over the last few weeks. "You... wanted to hear my voice?"

A light comes on, illuminating his face through the video feed.

Showing me sleepy brown eyes and bed head and a beard that's getting out of control.

"Turn on your light, baby," he murmurs and I lift my hand, lean over to turn on the bedside lamp. "There you are."

I inhale.

Because the words...God the way he says them. Soft and warm and beautiful and *wanted*.

"Hi," I whisper.

"Hey, beautiful," he says softly.

"It's early," I point out unnecessarily, earning a smile from him that is equally as lovely.

"Yeah, Sunlight."

"You should be sleeping."

"I will," he says. His smile turns a little self-deprecating. "Plus, you know I'll get my nap later."

"Such a baby," I tease, knowing all hockey players and their naps. "Did you bring your blankie with you too?"

A rustle and then the camera is panning down, showing a bare, heavily muscled chest that I've kissed my way across on full display. And then...it slides a little lower. "Yup."

I gasp. "Thief!"

The camera comes back up, centering on his gorgeous face, on the smile that's now fully teasing. "Told you."

The fuzzy blanket currently spread over half of that yummy torso is from *my* couch. "That's my favorite blanket," I say, narrowing my eyes.

"I know," he replies without a lick of remorse.

I glare at him.

He lifts the blanket, dragging the material toward his nose and sending my pulse skittering.

Because that lifting also gives me a glimpse of what's beneath.

And...*good morning*.

He inhales. "It smells like you, baby."

My lips part on a shaky exhale, heat blooming in my belly, need growing between my legs. "What happens when I'm sitting on my couch tonight and I get cold?"

The blanket settles back against his chest and I'm looking at his beautiful smile again. "I left you a present in return." He tucks a hand behind his head, putting that muscular arm with its full sleeve of tattoos on display. "Or *presents*, rather."

I frown, those words taking a second to process. "What?"

"Baby."

I blink, looking away from his arm, the tendrils of ink wrapped lovingly around it, and back into his eyes. "Yeah?"

"Go to the couch."

"Okay," I whisper, tossing back the blankets and getting out of bed. I pad across the carpet and out into the hall, flicking on lights as I go. Then I'm in my tiny living room, standing in front of my couch, seeing what I missed the night before. My blanket is gone.

Currently spread out on my sexy man's chest.

"Look behind the left side, baby."

My brows draw together, but I move to the side, bend down and...

Pull out a large gift bag.

How did I miss that?

"What's this?" I ask.

"Open it."

I tug the tissue paper free, reach inside, and—

"*Oh,*" I whisper, pulling the material out. It feels like silk, but it's not. It's heavier and fluffier than a cloud. Somehow both extremely soft and yet, I know it'll keep me warm. "It's lavender," I say softly.

"Your favorite color."

I freeze then shake my head and hold it closer. Of course he knows that.

"Wrap yourself up in it until I get back to do the job, yeah baby?"

It's just a blanket.

And it's so much fucking more than that.

"Yeah," I whisper.

"Good, Sunlight," he says so gently that my heart thuds again. "And then text me when you find the other presents I left you—"

"Why do you call me that?" I blurt.

I've never asked.

I couldn't know.

It would hurt too much when he...

Left me.

But the question is out there as I cling to a silky soft blanket in my favorite color that he's left for me.

And I'm invested in knowing the answer.

I'm *desperate* to know it.

Exhaling silently, I wait, eyes glued to his face, which has gone serious, his deep brown eyes boring into mine through the camera.

Part of me knowing that this explanation is going to change my life.

That it's going to mean something.

That it's—

"Because you're exactly that to me," he says, tone still gentle, *so* fucking gentle.

My pulse picks up, belly swirling, butterflies fluttering up to flap violently in the back of my throat.

"I was living in the shadows, baby. My life was—"

I inhale sharply, those butterflies stealing my words.

He's going to tell me, show me the hidden part of him, the piece of him that I've always known is there, but he's never given me. The proof that—at some point—he's going to leave. Because he needs to be with a woman with whom he can give that to.

A woman who isn't me.

But if he *does* give it...

Does that mean I can be her?

"I saw you sitting there beside your sister, looking shell-shocked, like your world had imploded, and I worried. I didn't know then that I didn't need to. That you're strong as hell. That you somehow keep on ticking even though the universe likes to pile too much shit on your plate. And despite that, when I showed up to help you with your mom and she was being"—he sits up, shoves a hand through his hair—"well, your mom..."

My lungs are tight. My vision is going black on the edges.

And I realize I haven't been breathing.

I exhale, inhale again. Repeat.

"And somehow, despite all the shit you've dealt with, despite your mom being a total bitch, you smiled at me." His eyes burn into mine. "You smiled at me and the shadows cleared and I *knew* that you were going to be the source of all the sunlight in my life. Of all the good things. Of anything that's going to mean anything."

"Oh," I whisper.

Because that's so beautiful, I can barely process it.

Because it's so beautiful, I can barely breathe.

He grins. "Cuddle that blanket close, baby. Cuddle that blanket and then kick ass at the bakery and in your classes, and know I'll be home soon."

"Okay," I say softly.

"Okay, my Sunlight," he murmurs. "Now, you need to get ready for your day."

He's right. I do.

But I find myself hesitating before saying, "Walker?"

A flash of a smile. "Yeah, baby?"

"What was your life like before?" I ask. "When it was filled with shadows."

His expression gentles, but the look in his eyes has disappointment settling in my belly.

Because I can already tell.

He's not going to give it to me.

"Dark," he says gently, and then as I absorb the blow of that soft brush-off, he adds, "There are three more presents hidden in your apartment. Text me when you find them." A beat, his mouth curving. "Now, though, I'm going to let you shower and get to work."

And I know.

I *know*...I'm not ever going to be that woman for him.

Twenty-Seven

I roll my shoulders then pick up a puck, carrying it around the ice, going through the motions in order to wake up my body.

We're not doing anything all that strenuous considering it's morning skate, and we have a game tonight. My group, in particular, is just focusing on some defensive positioning that'll be important against our opponents this evening and then I want to work on some set plays with my linemates, some one-timers because these fuckers are always on us in a second, and get some tips in.

After, we'll go back to the hotel for food and our afternoon nap.

Then warm-up and game and a flight back to Baltimore.

And—

"So, Dommie, huh?"

I blink, realize I've been skating around with the puck like a six-year-old, making slow, careful circles that definitely aren't worthy of a professional player, and one look at Smitty, who's leaning against the boards, beard out of control, grin wide, helmet half pushed back on his head tells me that my reprieve from the other day is over.

Smitty is locked in.

And I'm all aboard the gossip train.

Choo-choo!

Christ.

Grinding my back teeth together, I ignore him and continue with my warm-up.

But I know my fucking teammate isn't going to let me go.

Case in point—

"I know that Eva is the on-air personality, but Dommie is definitely the hot sister."

I spin in an instant, my stick hitting the ice with a *clink*, my gloves following suit, and then I'm launching myself at Smitty, not thinking logically—not at fucking *all*—because if I was, I wouldn't be hurling myself at my biggest and tallest and strongest teammate, wouldn't be going after a man whose punch is known around the league.

But I'm not thinking logically.

I'm on him in a second, and it's apparently faster than he expects because we collide and both go down hard (though, luckily for my ass, I'm the hockey player who ends up on top when we hit the ice).

His helmet goes flying, along with his stick and gloves, but I barely notice them because I'm gripping the front of his jersey and shaking him like a goddamned rag doll. "Don't you fucking talk about Dommie like that," I growl. "Don't you fucking *dare.*"

Smitty's still smiling, the fucker.

"Don't," I say again, feeling hands at my shoulder, distantly hearing my teammates telling me to calm down, to get off.

But they're not trying too hard.

They know I keep my shit locked down.

And they know it's likely that Smitty's stirring shit and deserves it.

"Don't fucking talk about her."

"Come on, man," Smitty says, still grinning. "You know you don't get a free pass, and you fucking know that everyone's going to be talking about you and her until there's something else to talk about."

"Jackson and Claire—" I begin, fully aware that I'm throwing them under the bus.

But there's a part of me that can't stop myself from doing it.

I have to protect Dommie. She doesn't need the scrutiny, doesn't need the extra attention and teasing. She's been through enough, especially with me giving her my special brand of asshole.

But even as I'm thinking that, I can't ignore that some part of me is also protecting myself.

Because if Smitty looks too closely, if the detectives on the Breakers start digging too deeply into my life, my past, my fucking present, they might—

Reasons.

I exhale, but Smitty's talking, distracting me from my panic.

"Jackson's not ready," he says, and tilts his head to the side, studying me far too fucking closely. "And I would say that neither are you, except for the fact that I'm currently sprawled on the ice because I called Dommie hot."

I growl.

Smitty grins. "Exactly. So," he says, "I'm not precisely sure that you *are* ready, but I am sure that your future is right the fuck in front of you, and that this is one of those occasions where you just have to put your fear aside and find a way to rise up to it."

"Kailey"—his newly pregnant wife—"know that you like to play inspirational speaker?" I mutter.

"Kailey's the one who tells me what to say."

I scowl. "Idiot."

He scowls. "Asshole."

"Right back at you."

"Right back at *you*—"

"And now I think we've come to the point in the festivities

where tempers have cooled, practice can continue, and then we can all fucking eat and take our naps," Jackson says dryly.

My lips twitch, but I don't look away from Smitty. Instead, I just shove him harder into the ice, know that it's going down the back of his jersey, soaking into his hair and not giving one fuck.

"Keep abusing me and you're going to get in trouble with my woman," Smitty says. "And she may be quiet, but she takes on dragons and mages and badass hockey players in her spare time"— they both play and bonded initially over the same video game— "so she won't like you beating up her baby daddy."

"She's got a whole team that can step in as baby daddies—"

Now it's Smitty's turn to growl.

And *my* turn to grin, despite the threat of violence entering the big man's face.

My amusement only lasts for a moment, though.

Because then I look up and I see cell phones pointed in my direction.

"Christ," I mutter, shoving Smitty one more time before crawling off him.

Smitty—very maturely (not that I'm taking *my* actions into account), promptly dumps me over. Ice shavings get in my hair, slide down the back of my jersey and I curse as I get up on my skates. "I am *so* telling Kailey what a shit-stirring asshole you are."

"You deserve it for the baby daddy bullshit," he mutters himself. "And you fucking know it."

I *do* know it.

Which is why I push my annoyance down and extend my hand toward him. "I know. She's yours the same way Dommie is mine."

"Damn right." He grabs my hand, pops up to his big ass feet, seemingly not giving one fuck that he's covered in snow. "And, Glitter, what you'll learn now that you've finally settled down and got yourself a good woman"—he shakes like a big fucking dog, sending melting snow in all directions and my teammates skittering away from the onslaught of wet and cold and back toward what we should all be doing, fucking *practicing*—"you'll get these women will love you through everything, even *when* you're an asshole."

I freeze.

Remain frozen as he skates away and joins the drills.

It's only Coach's whistle that snaps me out of it.

But my heart is still pounding as I skate toward my team.

Because I'm not sure if I'm more terrified to find out if that's bullshit...

Or if it's true.

Twenty-Eight

Dommie

"And I think you should take the lead for the stall at the arena."

I freeze, glance up from my notepad, heart suddenly in my throat. "What?"

"Come on, girlie," Ren, my boss—or former one anyway, since we've been partners for long enough that this meeting is two associates sitting down rather than me feeling like a little kid sent to the principal's office—says. "You know you can do it."

I know I can.

But...this is my boss. She's the one who laid the groundwork for the successful company that I've piggybacked onto.

The woman who saw a girl struggling and gave me an opportunity, a space to run my little side business, the chance to fold it into a larger more successful one when it started taking off.

The woman who easily could have taken advantage of me when I was young and inexperienced and naive, but instead...

Has always pushed me to do more, to believe in myself, to take that leap when I've hesitated on the cliffside.

So, it's no surprise she's pushing me now.

And...I think all of that past encouragement is the reason I know I can do this—because I've stepped into all facets of the shop and even when I've stumbled, I've figured my shit out, helped it become better than ever.

I can definitely headline the arena stall.

I've even already made the business plan for it.

One that Professor Bernard gave a perfect score.

So, I've created the sample menu, can bake all of the products as well as order the ingredients to make them. I can balance the accounts, run the point-of-sale system, hire employees to work the stall, even make an HR handbook.

I can do it all.

And my boss—my partner—knows this. "You've become the life of this place," she tells me. "People aren't here for my recipes—"

I frown. "Your recipes are what's kept this business open for over three decades."

Ren's white, permed curls bounce a little as she shakes her head, mouth curving. "Be that as it may, you're still the heart of this place."

I suck in a breath.

"And the brains," she says lightly, drawing another frown from me. "Let's face it, I've made more money since you've been in charge than I did over those two decades without you, girlie. You're the reason I've been able to take a vacation. You're the reason the line is out the door every day. You're the reason that we have good staff in place. I can say with utter certainty that you are the absolute best person who's ever stepped into this kitchen. Which is why," she adds before I can protest, leaning in and squeezing my hand, "I know you can take the lead at the arena. And why, if you do want to do it, I also think you need to start pulling back *here*."

The bakery needs me. "I can't—"

"You *can't* keep working six days a week and going to school *and* starting what is basically a brand new business at the arena.

You can't keep doing all of that *and* have a life." Her eyes take on a tinge of sadness that I know is the result of her divorce, and whether it was bakery-induced or that the bakery saved Ren from a dysfunctional relationship, my boss and partner has admitted to me before that she still doesn't know.

I *do* know that she worked long and hard over the years just to keep her head above water.

And that her personal life took a back burner because of that.

"This place gave me a lot," Ren says softly, "but it didn't give me everything. And I"—she sighs—"can't let you keep moving forward, thinking it will."

I shake my head. "I don't think that."

"Don't you?"

I pause, and she sees it.

"Because I'm worried you've allowed it to become a millstone instead of an opportunity."

My mouth opens. Closes.

"You don't have any decisions to make today"—she reaches out, takes my hand, squeezing it lightly—"I just want you to think about what you want. Because it doesn't *have* to be the bakery or the stall at the arena. It doesn't have to be what I want for you, or what everyone else wants for you, or something that makes you money. It doesn't even have to be because you stumbled onto a job you're extremely good at."

My throat goes tight and I can't force out a response because those words are hitting hard and low in my belly...just not where I would have expected them to hit.

I don't want this.

How many times have I thought that over the last months?

How many times have I shoved it aside and continued plowing forward?

"And," Ren says. "You can double down and make this your job, your career, your life, or you can dig deeper and change your mind and be something different." A pause. "Either are okay, so long as that's what you truly want."

"Ren," I whisper. "I don't know what to say."

"You don't need to say anything. You just need to find a quiet moment to think and make some decisions." Another squeeze of my hand. "And those decisions don't have to be the giant, scary ones. They can be about recipes and ingredients. Speaking of which..." She smiles before pivoting the conversation abruptly back to work.

I'm spinning, so I'm glad for the change.

Thankful for it.

I don't want this.

I *don't*.

"So, I know you're doing the menu, but I do have a few suggestions..." Her curls bounce again as she flips the page in her notebook.

Her suggestions are smart, steadying, perfect additions to the pieces I've been putting together.

Because Ren kicks ass.

Not just in the kitchen, either, I know as her words rattle through my brain when we finish up the meeting and she sends me off to class with a narrow-eyed expression that is a warning to think about my future.

The trouble is that I *have* been thinking.

I already know what I want—or what I *don't* want anyway.

I just don't know if I have the courage to go cliff diving.

———

Cool air clings to my cheeks as I walk to my car after class.

At best, snow is coming. At worst, it'll be freezing rain instead and I'll be navigating icy roads to the bakery at zero dark thirty tomorrow morning.

Fun times.

But the life of a baker.

Early mornings and long weeks and—

Except...it doesn't have to be that way, does it?

Ren's words have been flitting through my mind at regular intervals, settling heavier and heavier.

"Enough," I mutter when panic starts to crawl up my throat.

Even if I make the decision today, nothing is going to change right now. Plans have to be put into place. Baby steps need to be taken.

A life has to be built deliberately.

So says the woman who's clinging to scraps from a man who'll never trust me the way I need and—

"Enough."

I rub at my throbbing temple, take a deep breath, and force the thoughts out of my head.

Homework. Finalizing details for my stall at the arena.

Watching trash TV and bubble bath and—

My phone rings.

Frowning when I pull it out—because it's Walker's name on the screen and it's far too close to game time for him to be calling me—I quickly swipe and hold my breath as the video connects and his gorgeous face comes onto the screen.

"Hey, Sunlight."

And…everything is suddenly fine.

"Hi, honey," I say, digging into my purse for my keys.

"What's wrong?"

"Nothing," I tell him, pulling them out and holding them up to the camera. "I'm just about to get into my car."

His head tilts, eyes boring into mine. "That's not it."

I pause.

"Exactly," he mutters. "Now spill."

"It's not important." Just my whole life unsteady and ready to shatter when I've worked since I was sixteen to create stability and security and safety.

"Baby," he says. "Don't try to bullshit me. I can see right through that mask of yours."

I rub my throbbing temple again. "It's nothing. Really. Ren just said some things that got me thinking…"

"Thinking what?" he presses when I don't allow the rest of my thoughts to bubble up.

"It's close to game time," I hedge. "You don't have time to talk me through my existential crisis."

"You're thinking about quitting the bakery."

I inhale so sharply that I nearly choke on my own spit. "H-how do you know that?"

"*Everyone* knows it, Sunlight." His voice is gentle. "You're good at it, but you don't like it."

"I—" I shake my head. "No, it's fine. It's a good job and—"

"Your eyes die a little when you talk about going into work," he says. "I've seen it with guys in my profession. They're good at it, great at it, really, but they don't love it, and it ends up killing them slowly, inch by inch every single day."

My heart is throwing itself against my rib cage, and I can barely manage a breath. But I manage to squeeze out, "All jobs have their ups and downs." Yes, I'm still hedging. But *everyone* can see it? Christ. No wonder Ren gave me that spiel. And what could she think of me, hating—yes, there, I admitted it, *hating*—the job, hating being stuck there, hating that it feels like a pair of golden handcuffs because I'll never be good enough to find an equal or better opportunity—

"Dommie."

I blink, realize that I'm spiraling, that I'm completely zoning out.

"I think you need to have your existential crisis at my house," he says softly. "And not the dark"—he squints as though looking past me—"and mostly empty parking lot at school."

I glance around, my stomach clenching.

Shit.

It *is* dark and there are only a couple of people here.

"Time to get in your car, baby."

I nod, unlock the door, start to get in, but pause when I see the paper tucked under my wiper blade and straighten, leaning forward to snag it.

"What's that?" His voice is tense.

"Just an advertisement," I say without really looking at it, crumpling the paper and shoving it into the plastic pocket in my driver's side door, along with the many others I've collected over the last months. "I swear, I get one every time I park here."

His eyes are on mine for another long moment, but then he nods, orders gruffly, "Get your engine going, Sunlight. You look like you're shivering."

It's an order—and I'm inclined to bristle just because—but I *am* shivering, so I shove the keys into the ignition and crank up the heat.

"Lock the doors."

I narrow my eyes. "That's what I'm doing next."

His brows flick up. "So do it."

I hit the button.

"Good, baby."

I open my mouth to snap at him, but then I see the humor in his eyes, the way he's fighting a smile. "You're pushing it," I grumble.

"But now you're pissed at me instead of stuck in your own head."

I still, fingers clenching on my phone.

He's right.

Which is...

"You're annoying, you know that, right?"

A rough chuckle. "Yeah, baby, I do," he says lightly. But before I can reply to that, he adds, "Stay at my place, yeah?"

My brow furrows.

"I've got to go get ready to play in a minute." His tone is gentle. "And I'd really like to know that you're safe and warm and at a place with a full fridge you can raid."

I inhale. "I'm fine."

"I know you are," he says. "But really, you'd be doing me a favor."

My brows flick up in question.

"So I'm not worrying about you—and your existential crisis —during the game." His lips curve. "And it's quiet and you can watch the game on my big ass TV, and then late tonight, I can crawl into bed next to you and hold you."

My lungs inflate and I hold my breath for a second.

I'm tired.

And I want him to come home to me.

I want to soak in all of him I can, for as long as I can.

So...I just give in.

Twenty-Nine

I pull into the garage, wait for the heavy door to close behind me then turn off the ignition and get out.

It's after three and I'm exhausted.

But something—a wound, a worry, a deep, empty gorge inside me—fills in when I see Dommie's car parked next to mine, when I have the evidence of her here and safe.

Not placating me and then going home.

Not meeting me only part of the way and parking in the drive-way, ending up with a frozen windshield and a cold interior.

She's here.

I get out, round the trunk and reach into the back seat, grabbing my bag and the presents I picked up while on the road.

Her face when I gave her the blanket was burned into my soul. I will never, fucking *never* forget it.

And I'm going to do my best to make sure I see it as much as possible.

Especially, when her surprised and delighted texts over finding the box of underwear from the brand she loves and the expensive bubble bath I know she only uses for special occasions (and now has enough to use every day) were almost as good.

She needs spoiling.

And I'm the man to do it.

I start to head for the door to the house, but stop when I see a crumpled paper on the garage floor that's clearly fallen from Dommie's car. I pick it up, unfolding it, reading what's written inside.

Call me.

With a phone number scrawled below.

I scowl as I start forward again but shove down my irritation. At least it was crumpled up and discarded like the trash it is. Because if some asshole thinks he's going to get *my* woman...

Not fucking happening.

I reach the door and jiggle the handle, finding it locked. But I have the key and am glad that she listened to me on this front as well.

Safety fucking first.

Especially with my woman.

I punch in the code, hear the lock *whiz* as it retracts, and then move into the mud room. My bag goes on the hook, my dirties from my trip go in the washer, and then I grab the rest of my shit and Dommie's presents and head down the hall into the kitchen.

I'm expecting to leave the first present on the counter for her to find.

I'm *not* expecting to find *her* sitting in the kitchen, hair piled on top of her head, blanket wrapped around her shoulders, one knee tucked up beneath her chin. She's clutching the blanket closed and staring blankly off into space, dark circles illuminated by the under cabinet lights.

I freeze, gut churning, a fist reaching into my chest and clenching my heart tightly.

Because she looks so fucking lost.

And alone.

And—

I drop my shit on the island, set her presents carefully beside them, and then I'm next to her, crouching in front of her chair, cupping her jaw. "Baby," I say. "What's wrong?"

She blinks, shakes herself, eyes flying to mine. "Walker?" Her brows pull together. "What time is it—?" Her gaze flicks over my shoulder in the direction of the stove. "Oh my God, it's three in the morning and—"

Suddenly, she's a flurry of movement—tossing the blanket off, her leg sliding down and nearly unmanning me in the process. Then she's on her feet, and I'm following suit, popping up and grabbing her shoulders, steadying her as she bumps into the stool she was sitting on. I tug her back against my chest when she lurches forward. "Baby," I say. "Slow down. Take a breath. It's okay."

"It's not okay," she whispers. "I've been thinking all fucking night and I-I—" She exhales sharply. "Shit." She rubs at her temple. "I haven't slept and I have cakes to make today and—"

I spin her carefully in my hold, crouching again so I can meet her eyes. "Breathe, Sunlight. Just take a second and *breathe*."

Tears well up in her eyes and she shakes her head, but she *is* breathing, so I don't push her further, just keep her close, keep my breathing slow and steady, hoping that she'll match it. She does. Out. In. Hold. Out. In. Hold. Out. In. Hold.

Until the panic fades and her brow smooths out and guilt enters her eyes.

"What?" I whisper.

"You're probably tired and want to go to bed." She tries to step back, but I move with her, keeping my chest pressed to hers, our legs intermingled. "I'm not sleeping, so I should just go into work and—"

"Yeah, no," I say. "That's not happening."

Her brows yank together, forming a sharp V.

"You're not going into work when you have haven't slept."

"First, you don't get to tell me what to do," she snaps. "And second, I have cakes to bake and cases to fill and—"

"Someone else can do that today," I say, moving closer, pressing her back against the island. "Today, you need to get some sleep and—"

"I have responsibilities," she says, shaking her head and pushing at my chest, trying to slip by me. "I can't leave them in a lurch."

I study her face, seeing the stubbornness written into the lines of her face, and I know I don't have a chance at winning this one.

"Fine," I tell her, stepping back and snagging my keys from the island. "Let's go."

A slow blink. "What are you talking about?"

I shove one arm into my jacket and then the other. "I'm not sending you out onto the roads with no sleep and a full day of work ahead of you."

"I *have* to work," she says quietly.

"Yeah," I say, making it clear in my tone that I know that she's peddling bullshit. "And I'm taking you."

"I—"

I hold up my keys. "Do you need to change first?"

———

She's pissed.

I'm exhausted, and pissed that she's pissed.

But I'm not going anywhere.

Even though she fought me about getting changed and fought me about driving her here. Even though she then fought me and tried to get me to go home once I *did* get her here.

Even though she's now stopped fighting me and is giving me the silent treatment.

Lucky for me, she's made it stupid proof for her employees, so I can help her, even despite the taut silence in the kitchen.

Of course, I'm slow as fuck as I measure out dry ingredients, still working on one laminated recipe card while she's torn through enough of them in the hours we've been here so that the space is warm and filled with delicious smells and the cases out front are practically overflowing.

"So," I say, attempting to break the silence for the umpteenth time, "about that existential crisis…"

She freezes, wisps of her dark hair escaping her ponytail and curling around her face, and her eyes narrow. "You're not funny."

"Well," I say, "that *is* Smitty's role in the locker room." A beat. "And speaking of Smitty…"

She starts dumping butter into a mixer, turns it up to full speed, clearly trying to drown out the sound of my voice.

I add a few more scoops of flour to the bowl on the scale until it's at the proper weight and then set it aside so that I can move onto the next ingredient. But before I do, I move across the kitchen, stop in front of her and turn off the mixer. "He knows about us," I say softly. "Which means the entire team knows about us. Which means…" I lift my brows. "Your sister is going to —or already *does* know about us."

"My sister"—she sighs—"Eva probably knew about us months ago. She's just too smart to truly push me on it."

"Because you're stubborn."

"So says the man who's so closed down that he's barely shared anything about himself with me."

My brows fly up. and I still as ice shoots through my veins.

I open my mouth, not sure what I'm going to say—even though I know I *have* to say something, but I don't get so much as a syllable out.

Because the bell dings out front.

An angry voice rings out.

And all hell breaks loose.

Thirty

"What the actual fuck?" Ren snaps as the swinging door to the kitchen explodes open, slamming into the wall and nearly making me upend the bowl of butter I'm carefully adding to the mixer.

I clutch at the smooth metal edges, manage to not drop it on the floor—or into the mixing bowl all at once—and turn toward my boss, my partner.

Her scowl is as ferocious as the time I nearly smoked out the front of house because I forgot about a tray of croissants in the oven.

I don't remember if I cried more because all that hard work was ruined, or because Ren was so pissed at me.

Today, I already feel my pulse speeding up, my throat tightening, nausea roiling in my stomach.

It's the I've fucked up, the walk down the school corridor to the principal's office feeling.

The I'm going to lose *everything* feeling.

The—

Ren stomps across the floor, her boots loud on the tile,

her coat swinging behind her. Then she stops, seems to realize that Walker is standing next to me, an apron that is comically small tied around his big body. "New assistant?" she asks dryly.

"Something like that," Walker says, extending his hand and introducing himself.

"Oh, I know who you are," Ren mutters. "Seeing as this isn't the first time you've stormed into my kitchen."

There's only one person storming, and it's not Walker.

Not unless she's talking about storming my defenses.

Because the man blew right by them long ago.

"Well," Walker says, seemingly not bothered by Ren's icy tone, "that's because there are beautiful women who inhabit this kitchen."

Ren snorts then turns her back dismissively on Walker, who seemingly doesn't take offense if his lips turning up is any indication. Then my former boss is in my face, her brows flicking up in question.

"What?" I ask softly.

"Is there a reason you're standing in this kitchen an hour earlier than you're supposed to *begin* baking with dark circles under your eyes and the cases already full—which means that you've been here hours already?"

"Yeah," Walker says before I can come up with an excuse to put Ren off, "because she didn't sleep last night and refused to let me take her to bed when I got home."

Ren's brows climb higher and she slowly spins away from me. "Explain."

I choke out a protest, but both of them ignore me.

"I got home from my flight a couple of hours ago. She was awake, hadn't slept all night." Ren slants a glance over her shoulder at me. "And instead of calling in someone to cover for her"—Ren's face changes before she looks away again, focus going back to Walker—"she insisted on coming to the bakery early." A beat. "And without sleep."

Ren rotates back toward me, and those lifted brows speak volumes.

I nibble at my bottom lip.

"*Without* sleep?" Ren asks archly.

I nibble harder.

Ren sighs and shakes her head. "I was hoping that I wouldn't have to do this."

"D-do what?" I ask, fear threatening to steal my voice as I clench at the edges of the bowl.

"You're fired."

My mouth falls open. "I— But—" I clear my throat. "You can't do that."

We're partners. We can't just cut the other one out.

"You're right," Ren says. "I can't fire you outright. But I *can* kick you out of the day-to-day operations here at the bakery."

My inhalation is sharp.

Because she's right.

Our contract says exactly that.

Profits were to be split equally, but this space is hers and she gets the final say in control of the bakery and its employees.

I just...I never thought that she would use it.

Because she's always treated me as her equal.

Ren reaches out and carefully extracts the bowl from my grip, sets it on the counter with a soft *clang*. "Please get some rest and take some time for yourself," she says gently.

My eyes slide closed.

"And when you're ready, focus on the stall at the arena, on your classes." A squeeze that has my lids peeling back. "Focus on *you* and—" Her eyes flick to the side, toward Walker. "Focus on thinking about what you want for your future."

My belly contracts.

"And I mean this in the nicest possible way," she says, "but I don't want to see you back here until you've done all of that focusing for at least two weeks."

Two *weeks?*

That's a freaking eternity. "But we have cakes to bake and decorate and that event at the museum—"

"I don't know if you remember," Ren says a little sharply, "but I *did* run this place by myself for two decades. I can bake the cakes and we have plenty of staff to help me with the event."

Staff I would likely not use to their full potential because I'm a freaking control freak and have to do everything myself.

God, I'm an asshole.

I wince. "I didn't mean you couldn't—"

"I know," she says softly.

"I just..." I nibble at my bottom lip again. "What am I going to do if I'm not working?"

Who am I going to be?

Ren flicks her stare toward Walker, mouth curving. "I have an idea of what you can do—or *who*, rather," she says silkily. But even as my cheeks flare with heat she lifts her hand up, palm out, fingers twitching. "Apron please."

My fingers clench into fists at my sides. "Wh-what?"

She moves toward me, tugs at the string on the knot holding my coverall in place. "Apron," she says again, slipping it over my head and hanging it on her arm before she moves to Walker. "You too, big guy."

Walker obediently unties his apron, then pulls it off and passes it over to Ren.

"Good," Ren mutters walking them to the hooks on the far side of the kitchen and hanging them up. "Now go home, Dommie," she says quietly, pulling on her own apron, wrapping the strings behind her, tying them in front. "Go home and do nothing." Half of her mouth turns up. "Nothing except your big, scowly hockey player, that is."

She disappears down the hall, moving toward the office.

Walker chuckles, but his laughter immediately cuts off when I shoot my stare—okay, my *glare*—in his direction.

Then he seems to get a look at my face—a real look—because he's at my side in a second, wrapping his arm around my shoulders, pulling me against him, burying my face into the base of his throat.

My breath hitches, and his hand settles gently on the back of my head. "Chin up, Sunlight," he says as his other arm wraps around me and he hugs me tight. "It'll be okay."

I'm scared and embarrassed, freaked way the fuck out and...

I'm maybe a little relieved that Ren made the call for me, that I don't have to make the decision to not be here—for a couple of weeks anyway.

But I also feel as though my tether has been cut and I'm drifting away.

I don't have to be here, so where do I have to be now?

I don't have to be here, so what am I?

I don't have to—

"Come on, baby," Walker says, adjusting his hold, turning me so his arm is around my shoulders and I'm tucked into his side as he starts walking forward.

"I don't know what I'm doing," I whisper.

"I know," he tells me quietly. "But I know the place to go to figure it out."

Thirty-One

Donna's pancakes have a way of helping people find clarity.

They're magic, I swear.

But sitting across the booth from Dommie as she devours a banana nut stack—banana-flavored pancakes with toasted almonds and freshly whipped cream—is as magical for me as the restorative properties of those tasty carbs appear to be for her.

Those circles are still far too fucking dark, and I'm barely resisting the urge to bundle her out of here, drive her home, and keep her locked up in my bed for the next twelve hours, but the paleness is gone and she's actually eating, despite protesting that she wasn't hungry from the moment we walked through the door.

Luckily, I know her.

And I know what she likes.

And I've eaten here enough to make a perfect match between the two.

My phone buzzes and I glance down at the screen, frowning at the unknown number, my heart suddenly in my throat, but I dismiss the call, shove it back into my pocket.

"You probably think I'm ridiculous," she whispers into her pancakes.

I frown. "What are you talking about, baby?"

"I'm a grown woman and I don't know what I'm doing, and you just saw Ren fire—" She breaks off, shoves a huge bite of pancakes into her mouth.

Suddenly not hungry, I push my own plate away from me, slide out of the booth, and shove myself into the other side, crowding into her. "Hey," I say gently, not missing the tears shining in her eyes. "*Hey*, Sunlight. It's okay."

She drops her fork to her plate. "How is it okay? I'm waffling about a job I don't like, and it's so obvious my boss just tried to fire me."

I set my hand onto the back of her neck, squeeze lightly. "You know that's not what just happened."

"Isn't it?" she asks, voice so quiet I have to lean close to hear it. "Everyone seems to see inside my head better than me."

"Sometimes it's easier to see something when you're at a distance from it."

She picks up her fork again, jabs at the pancakes, but she's not eating them any longer. "I'm not sure that's true," she mutters. "You seem to know exactly what you want. Eva didn't need anyone to figure out her path, and neither did Gabe."

"And does Jer taking a year to figure out his future mean that he's some sort of failure?"

"No, of course not, but he's a baby. He hasn't had time to sort out his future."

"And you have?"

Her fork hits the plate again. "I'm twenty-six."

"But you've been in survival mode for the last decade, baby. You've been so focused on getting through and helping Eva put food on the table and taking care of your brothers and your mom and not squandering the opportunity of Dommie's Cakes that you haven't had a second to stop and think about what you wanted."

She freezes.

"And it's not until the opportunity at the arena came up," I say, giving her my best guess of what had happened, considering when I first noticed the conflict and guilt and indecision appear in her eyes. "It's not until then that you really felt the walls closing in on you. Because until then you could just quit the bakery, but if you start opening up multiple locations, leaving becomes harder and harder until eventually you're stuck."

Her throat works and then her head slowly turns, giving me a glimpse of her wide brown eyes. "I don't know what to say," she whispers.

"Because I'm really wrong? Or really right?"

A breath that has her shoulders rising and falling. "Really freaking right."

Her tone has me relaxing slightly. Because she's gritted that out, sass and irritation coming back, sadness fading away.

Her eyes practically blaze up at me. "Why in the fuck is it that you could see all that and I'm standing on the sidelines of my life just flapping my arms like a useless idiot?"

I cup her jaw. "Survival mode, baby." And I'd be lying if her comment back at the bakery didn't prime my following words. "I grew up living it."

Her expression gentles. "You did?"

I want to change the topic of conversation. I want to avoid it all together.

But...she needs this.

And I know I'm the only one who can give it to her.

"My parents weren't exactly functional."

More gentling. "What do you mean?"

Run. Avoid. Change the subject.

Only I can't.

Because if I don't give her this then she'll keep on thinking...

This woman I love so *fucking* much will continue thinking that I don't care about her enough to share what's inside *my* head.

So, I do the only thing I can.

I give her more.

"Mine isn't an uncommon story," I murmur. "I'm the product of a toxic relationship between two young people. One that resulted in my mom getting pregnant and—no surprise—my good old dad skipped out on responsibilities, both financial and emotional."

Her head jerks, hand lifting to cover mine where it still cupped her jaw. "I'm sorry."

"It's what it is." I shrug. "We didn't have a lot, but life was pretty good until my mom found out that my dad had hit it big and went after him for child support." A beat. "He should have paid it—I knew that much even them, but he didn't go down without a fight and neither did my mom. He wanted to give less. She wanted more. And"—I slip my hand out from under hers—"all of that meant I spent most of my formative years as a pawn for them to fuck each other over."

"Honey," Dommie whispers.

"It's fine, baby," I say. "I promise. They're both alive and have plenty of money and still hate each other." I force a smile. "The bonus is that I now play for a team that is located on the opposite coast, so I only see them for the odd day here or there."

"Breeze in and breeze out."

My stomach twists. "What?"

"I heard you tell Theo that the last time you guys were playing the Sierra—that you were going breeze in and breeze out."

I inhale, hold that breath for long enough that my lungs begin to protest.

Then I give in and let it slide out. "Yeah, baby," I say. "It's the only way I can survive being in the same room as either of them to this day. Short visits with easy escape routes."

Her eyes are glittering with tears again, and I hate that she's feeling that for me, especially when it's *way* in the past, when I'm over it—and have been over it for fucking years now. "I hate that for you," she whispers.

"It's over now and I'm fine."

Those shining eyes tell me that she doesn't buy my prevarication, and her words prove it. "Walker, I don't think it's that easy."

It's not easy.

It's why I fucked up with Dommie in the first place, why I have so much to make up for.

But it's the past—done, over, dealt with, moving the fuck on.

"It's fine, baby," I say. "I'm only bringing it up now so you know that I get it, that no one who loves you will judge you for not being a hundred percent certain of what you want to do with your life, especially since you've spent so long just trying to continue putting one foot in front of the other."

She stills. "Loves me?"

I still.

Rewind back through my words and realize what I said.

I was planning on waiting to tell her, waiting until things settle more, until she trusts me completely.

So, obviously, I don't need to rewind through my feelings.

Not when they're right there, have been there for ages, blazing lights on a giant billboard.

And now she's looking up at me with those soft, soft eyes.

"Sunlight," I say. "I lo—"

"Well, look who we have here!"

Thirty-Two

Dommie

Smitty's voice has Walker cursing and turning away from me.

It almost has *me* cursing.

Because he'd said *loved*—

"Banana nut," Smitty booms, sliding into the booth opposite of me. "Good choice. And Glitter, man, the menu is fucking twenty pages, do you ever order anything different?"

"When I know what I want," Walker grits out, glaring over at Smitty, "I'm smart enough to keep it."

My heart flutters.

Keep me.

Keep *me.*

Love me?

But maybe—?

"Hey, Connor," the server Betty, a plump older woman with a pen tucked behind her ear, says, "what'll it be today, honey?"

"He's not staying," Walker grinds out.

The woman turns her head toward us and lifts her brows, but

doesn't blink an eye when Smitty reclines back into "his" side of the booth and grins as he puts in his order for more food than I could eat in a lifetime. Betty—probably very familiar with the shenanigans of the Breakers crew—doesn't falter, just ignores Walker's grumbling, writes down Smitty's very large order and, asks me if I want a refill on my hot chocolate.

I nod. "Thanks."

"Just doing my job, sweetheart," she says and turns toward Smitty, telling him she'll bring his coffee right over.

"Decaf," Smitty says and thanks her.

"Got it." Then she's striding away with a wink at me and a placating smile tossed in Walker's direction.

Probably knowing that fighting against the hurricane that is Smitty is a lesson in futility.

"So Little Moreno," Smitty says, his body taking up the vast majority of the other bench, "what do you see in our Walker here?"

Walker growls and my hand settles on his thigh, squeezing lightly. "How's Kailey feeling?" I ask, going for diversion before my man reaches his breaking point.

Smitty immediately softens, and—that right there—is why everyone loves the big man despite the fact that he's a gossip monger and a shit-stirrer.

He loves his woman.

Would lay his big body down to protect her.

Hell, he'd do that for anyone he cares about—which includes his teammates, their significant others, and the team's support staff. Which also includes Eva, and because Eva loves me it also includes...me.

I'm part of the Breakers family.

Somehow.

And that's why I can see through the relaxed, teasing demeanor, and feel the careful way he's studying me.

Making sure I'm okay.

Even though he doesn't have any obligation to do so.

"She feels like shit," he says. "Tired and nauseous all the time, but she's feeling better this morning and wanted pancakes and coffee. But she'll be here soon. She just made a pitstop in the bathroom and sent me on ahead when I spotted you two."

Well, that explains why he ordered so much.

But sent him on ahead. *Ha*.

More than likely his gossip radar pinged and he couldn't stay away.

Smitty winks at me as Betty fills two mugs with decaf, and then Kailey's at the table, her color a little pale, but her face as warm and soft with love as Smitty's is.

"Thanks, honey," she tells Smitty quietly—their two demeanors can't be more different, she is soft-spoken and shy, and Smitty's presence fills every space he enters. She looks up at me, gentle smile on her face. "Do you need me to wrangle the beast to another table so you two can have privacy?"

"Yes," Walker mutters.

"No," I say at the same time.

Walker glances down at me, eyes sparking, but when I just squeeze his thigh again, he sighs and shakes his head...

But I see something else.

Something that has my belly filling with butterflies.

Because there's soft there too.

For me.

I inhale sharply, but Walker is shifting, sliding his arm around my shoulders, clearly settling in for the long haul.

Because *I* want him too.

More butterflies.

It's not until later, after Kailey and Smitty have devoured their stacks of pancakes—and after Kailey tiptoes into the conversation and shows how smart and funny and wonderful she is—that a yawn escapes despite my best effort to ignore the fatigue pulling at my bones.

And that's when something big and bright and hopeful blazes through me.

Because no sooner has that yawn escaped me before Walker's up and out of the booth, reaching into his wallet and tossing some bills on the table. He's grabbing my hand a moment later, tugging me off the leather-covered bench and, barely giving me a second to say goodbye before he's shuttling me toward the exit.

"Bye, Glitter!" Smitty booms. "And just saying, Eva's going to *love* how you're looking after her little sister."

I almost trip, but Walker's arm around my waist keeps me upright, and he doesn't miss a beat as he lifts his free hand, middle finger extended.

Smitty's laughter rings out.

Then we're pushing through the door, the cold winter air a slap in the face.

It only lasts for a second before I'm tucked closer to Walker's warm frame, and then I'm being bundled into his car, my seat belt pulled across my body.

Click.

A hand on my cheek. "Sleep time, Sunlight."

Almost on cue, another yawn slides through my body.

Walker smiles gently at me.

As gently as Smitty smiled at Kailey.

Hope blazed through me, bright and beautiful and *wonderful*.

He presses a kiss to my forehead.

And then he drives me back home.

———

I wake up sweating, heat scorching my back, a heavy weight slung across my middle.

I inch my feet toward the edge of the comforter, seeking a sliver of coolness while still trapped in the inferno that is Walker holding me while I sleep.

Ah.

I almost sigh in relief when the air hits my bare skin.

The man can start a fire, just by cuddling.

The sun is high outside the windows, which means that we likely didn't sleep enough, but it's bright enough that I know there's no chance of me going back to sleep.

So, I just lay there for a while, thinking about Ren and work and the forced two-week hiatus.

Eventually, though, nature calls and I try to slowly creep my way to the edge of the mattress—and I'm about as successful in escaping as the previous time I attempted this.

Which is to say, not at all.

One second, brisk air is coating my skin and the next I'm being pressed into the mattress by that big, scorching body, Walker's sleeping face in my mine, his big, hot hand slipping beneath his T-shirt I'm wearing to sleep in.

It slides up along my side, sending goose bumps prickling along my skin. "Where do you think you're going?" he rumbles.

My mouth curves.

Because we've played this out before.

Because he's so tuned into me and my body that he notices me slipping out of bed.

Because...he doesn't want me to go.

"Bathroom," I tell him, arching against his touch, nature's call suddenly very far away.

"Hmm," he says, bending and burying his nose in my throat. "This is becoming a problem."

My chuckle is startled. "My having to go to the bathroom is a problem?"

A nip of his teeth. "Mmm-hmm."

"You've lost your mind."

His tongue flicks out. "Maybe."

I chuckle again, but this time it breaks off into a sigh of contentment when his lips continue moving, sliding along my throat, teasing and soft. I sling my leg around his hip, start rocking against him.

He groans, hand shifting, cupping my breast, and then I'm the one who's groaning.

Who's grinding.

Who's suddenly desperate to have him inside me.

Thirty-Three

I sense the change in her.

The melting of her body beneath mine, the way her breathing hitches, how her fingers wind through my hair, gripping tightly.

Pinpricks of pain through my scalp.

Heat arrowing toward my cock.

I want to tug off her underwear and plunge inside her.

She'll welcome me.

I know it.

She'll enjoy it.

I also know that I can make it good for her any and every time.

But—

I flop over onto my back, bringing her with me and tangling us both in the blankets.

She squeaks out a protest, but then she's atop me, legs straddling my waist, the hard length of my dick pressing against the thin fabric covering her pussy, fabric that would be easy to tug to the side.

Slick evidence of her arousal on my fingertips, on the head of my cock.

The tight, hot clasp of her pussy around me as I plunge deep—

So not helpful when she has a more pressing need than me fucking her into oblivion.

"Go," I manage to rasp out, yanking the blankets from around us, tossing them to the side, and swatting her butt.

Her eyes are bleary, her expression is so fucking confused it's adorable. "What?" she whispers, her hands coming to rest on my bare chest.

I grunt and sit up, swooping her against me as I plunk my feet onto the rug and carry her into the bathroom. "Go on, baby," I murmur, swatting her sexy ass again before I turn around and walk out, closing the door behind me.

My stomach rumbles, protesting that we've missed lunch and I mentally begin cataloging the food in my fridge and pantry. Surely, I can come up with some sort of—

"You coming?"

The sultry tone of her voice is like a hand wrapping around my cock, stroking hard.

I spin around, nearly choke when I find the door open and her standing there, one arm up, fingers gripping the wooden frame.

Naked.

She's standing there naked, rosy tips of her breasts hard and calling for my mouth. I want to suck on them until they turn bright pink, like raspberries, then drop to my knees, kissing my way along the curve of her belly, down toward the patch of dark curls at the apex of her thighs.

Then I realize I can.

Forgetting about the contents of my fridge, I stalk toward her, loving the way the pace of her breathing increases. Loving her gasp as I bend, bypassing her mouth and sealing my lips around one begging nipple, sucking deeply, feeling the sting of her nails on my scalp. But I don't stop—just keep suckling and kneading her flesh, using my free hand to pluck at her other nipple.

"Oh God," she whispers, drawing me closer, her body undulating against mine, her leg lifting—

I capture it, tossing it over my shoulder and not waiting to bury my face in her pussy. I thrust my tongue inside her, use my nose to put pressure on her clit, and then she's moaning and grinding against me, threatening to suffocate me in that sopping cunt, but I don't stop fucking her with my mouth, don't stop until I know that she's *right there.*

Dipping one foot over the edge.

Only *then* do I pull back.

Only then do I scoop her up and carry her to the bed, dropping her onto the edge of the mattress, leaning over her and taking her mouth in a deep, wet kiss.

I know she can taste herself and that nearly sends my control splintering.

But I hang on.

Only then she wraps her legs around my waist and that slick heat brushes the head of my cock and—

Red hazes the edges of my vision.

It takes every bit of strength I possess to not flex my hips, to not slide into that wet clasp. I reach for my wallet—

"It's okay to forget the condom," she murmurs. "I have the shot."

I still, cold sliding down my spine.

Because there was another time, another woman who had said that.

And that had led to...

Reasons.

Shuddering, I push up from the bed so quickly that her legs fly from around my waist, flop down to the mattress.

Her eyes are wide, her mouth dropping open. "Are you ok—"

Ding dong!

"Shit," I mutter.

"Ignore it," she says, sitting up and reaching for me.

I flinch back.

I can't help it.

I just...*do.*

And the pain rippling across her face is one of the worst things I've ever seen.

That's enough to snap me out of my shit, to slap me across the back the head, to remind me that the woman in my bed is much, much different from any of the others who have ever been in my life.

Dommie is mine.

Forever.

"What's hurting you?" she asks softly.

"Nothing." I shake my head, watching as pain slices through her again. Fuck. I can't do this. I have to tell her everything and—

Ding dong!

"Christ," I mutter as the doorbell goes again, as it's paired with knocking that's loud enough it makes its way upstairs.

Knocking that can only signify one thing.

A teammate.

Or...

No, *she's* not coming back.

Dommie reaches forward and I hate that the way she extends her arm is so damned tentative, as though she's putting herself within striking distance of a snake.

I clench my teeth, dig my toes into the rug beneath the bed, but I. Don't. Fucking. Move.

Her fingers brush along my chest.

Her palm presses over my heart. "Trust me," she whispers as the organ pounds beneath. "Please, Walker, I've told you—" A shake of her head. "You know what's in my mind. You've seen—"

Ding dong!

Knock! Knock! KNOCK!

"Please just tell me."

I shake my head.

I stop that movement a fraction of a second later, but she clocks it—the reticence and fear and *reasons* I'm keeping from her.

She stills for a moment, watching me, brown eyes swimming with hurt. Then she sighs and drops her hand away.

The sudden cold that grips me is like I've just plunged into an ice bath—it's all-encompassing and frozen and...terrifying.

I push that down, unclench my hands, intending to grab her, to tell her something, anything, maybe—my throat closes up—*everything.*

Ding dong! Ding dong! Ding dong!

She shifts to the side, moving away from me, moving out of reach.

Or maybe the fear that rises up is so strong that...

I let her go.

Either way, she's off the bed, padding into the bathroom, the door closing firmly behind her.

The lock *snicking* as it's engaged.

KNOCK! KNOCK! KNOCK!

"Fuck!" I snap, shoving a hand through my hair, indecision filling every cell of my body. I need to tell her.

I *can't.*

I'll lose her if I don't.

But...I fucking *can't.*

"You're a goddamned idiot, Walker," I mutter as I stomp over to my dresser, yanking open the top drawer and pulling out a pair of sweats, tugging them on before I storm out of the bedroom and pound down the stairs.

I'm going to kill whoever the fuck is on the other side of it—because it's easier to kill them, to be pissed at them instead of myself.

Or maybe it's easy to be pissed at the world because I'm so fucked up.

Ding dong! Ding dong! KNOCK! KNOCK! KNOCK!

"Fucking assholes," I grind out as I close in on the front door. "We are all motherfucking ass—"

I whip the door open, intending to finish the curse for my annoying as fuck teammates' ears, intending to turn the air so fucking blue the bastards are going to get frostbite.

But the words stopper up in my throat.

Because it's not my teammates standing on my front porch.

Or not *only* them.

Because they're crowded behind one...

Eva Moreno.

And the former reporter looks ready to interrogate me.

Thirty-Four

Dommie

I'm sitting on the edge of the tub, hurt slicing through me before I remember myself.

Remember the person I'm working on becoming.

"Fuck this," I whisper, shoving the pain down, pushing away the urge to ball myself up, to make myself small.

Walker said that I was the brightness that brought him out of the shadows.

Ren said I needed to value myself.

They've both told me over and over to go after what I want.

Well, what I *want* is a relationship where I'm a fucking equal, where the man I love—yes *love,* because why would I put myself through this angst otherwise, why would his breaking up with me months ago have hurt so much if I didn't love him. I want the man I love to value me enough, to trust me enough, to *love* me enough to give me every part of him.

Because I want to offer the same up to him on a silver platter.

Because I want to know him as well as he knows me.

Because—

"I'm done with this fucking shit."

Done with dimming my light.

I'm going to burn bright, going to blaze like a fucking inferno.

I'm going to be me—and I'm grabbing on to all the things I deserve, holding fucking tight and—

I pop to my feet and reach for Walker's T-shirt. Then I'm out of the bathroom, prepared for a fight...only to find the bedroom empty.

Right.

The doorbell. And the copious amount of knocking.

And...I'm not wearing any underwear.

I stop, turn away from the door I'd been intending on storming through, prepared—for once in my life—to pick a fight, to demand what I deserve.

To blaze like the motherfucking sun.

Voices ring up through the floor, and I'm very glad I haven't actually made it through the door.

Blazing can wait until I have pants on.

Despite myself, I smile.

Probably better than shooting laser eyes at Walker, especially if we have company. Which is a thought that prompts me to turn around and search the room for my clothes.

I wasn't very coherent when we returned from having pancakes—a combination of exhaustion and yummy carb overload.

"Ah," I whisper, spotting the pile of clothing crumpled up next to the side of the bed.

Where I left them after Walker pulled his tee over my head.

Speaking of which...I take off that T-shirt, toss it onto the bed then stride back into the bathroom, snag my undies, and focus on getting dressed, on keeping my courage.

On—

"Being motherfucking Sunlight," I mutter to my reflection, giving myself a firm, but encouraging nod.

Then I put my pants on.

———

"Oh my God," my sister says patting her stomach after having put away so much—*so much*—of the pizza that Walker made.

Yup. *Made.*

For the six people who crashed our day off together—Eva and Theo, Pru and Marcel, and Raph and Beth. I only assume that Smitty wasn't here because he already got a good look at the show this morning, and didn't need any further fodder for his gossip channels.

Walker wasn't happy about the intrusion, but he didn't send them away, either.

And, I have to admit, it's been nice.

Really nice to sit and eat and drink and just...be in the present without worrying about homework and deadlines and cakes that need to be filled with delicious beauty.

It was *really* nice to eat something I didn't make, especially when it was a yummy homemade pizza that included dough Walker made from scratch and a spicy honey that I want to lick off his naked body.

Will lick off his naked body.

If only he'll look at me.

But he's gotten increasingly quiet. And distant. Especially after everyone except for Theo and Eva left.

Though maybe that's because my sister cornered me and demanded details, extremely unhappy that I hadn't looped her into every private detail of my life.

"Do you want to take the rest of this home?" I ask, having already filled a zip-top with leftovers for Walker and me.

"Um, a thousand times yes, my baby sis."

I roll my eyes, but I do it smiling...*and* filling up a bag for her and Theo, and then as though conjured by my thoughts—or maybe because he's taken pity on me and is sacrificing himself to save me from my nosy sister, Theo moves into the kitchen, loops an arm around Eva's chest and murmurs something in my sis's ear that turns her cheeks scarlet.

"I'll just grab our stuff," he says, winking at me after he straightens, lifting his lips from her ear. "Want me to pretend to warm up the car so you can interrogate your sister further?" he asks Eva.

I glare.

"Of course I do," Eva says.

More glaring. So much for sacrificing himself.

He just laughs and kisses the top of my head before striding out of the room.

Eva sighs contentedly. "God, I love my man."

I roll my eyes, but I'm happy for her—and happy to almost have the house empty so I can do what I intended before the Breakers family descended: get Walker's head straight. "Come on, sissy," I say. "With or without your hubby's delay tactics, it's time for us to pack this in."

She follows me out the front door and waits as I tuck the bag of leftovers into the trunk of her car. Something feels off, but I can't pinpoint it as I straighten, rub at the prickly feeling on my nape, and glance over my shoulder.

I search the shadows, the bushes, the other cars parked on the street, but don't see anything out of the ordinary.

Clearly, I've been watching too many scary movies.

The imagination is a powerful thing.

I narrow my eyes, giving the area a final survey, but there's no one there—

Or no one there except the two remaining hockey players who are unabashedly watching us from the front porch while we finish up our sisterly moment.

"What is it?" Eva asks when I look over my shoulder again.

"Nothing," I say, forcing a smile and returning my focus to my sis. "Except that—all things considered—" And what she interrupted. "I'm glad you swung by."

A snort. "Sure you are."

"I mean it, sissy," I tell her. "I—" I take a breath and another step toward the person I want to be. "I've been in crisis for so long that I didn't feel like I could stop and enjoy moments like tonight. So—" I exhale. "It *is* nice that you're here, that you and Walker and Ren and the rest of the guys are forcing me to stop and actually enjoy my life instead of plowing forward toward the next thing I have to deal with."

Her face goes stark. "Dommie, I—"

I touch her cheek. "I didn't know that's what I was doing, that I wasn't really living. It was just...survival mode until I was too burned out to enjoy anything, to think clearly, to...actually do something more than just exist."

"Honey," she whispers, taking my hand. "I hate that for you."

"I hate it for me too," I say—or *now* I do anyway. Before it had just been...reality.

But things are different. I might not have all the answers, but I'm learning and I'm not going back to the person I was, to the life I thought was all I could have.

"No more," Eva whispers.

I nod. "Not ever again."

Her fingers squeeze mine. "Good, sissy."

We fall quiet for a moment before she straightens her shoulders and pops her lips. "Well, now that you're turning over a new leaf, you'd better get used to me showing up unannounced."

"Yeah, no." I nudge her arm. "That's not what I've given you permission to do. You can call or text first."

She taps a finger to her mouth. "Hmm. I do have that spare key."

"You wouldn't," I say, narrowing my eyes.

Her lips twitch. "I have to look after my baby sister."

"Eva," I warn.

It's a warning she ignores as she leans in and squeezes me tightly. "Love you, knucklehead."

"Rude," I mutter. "And after I'm finally figuring out how to look after myself."

She pulls back, gives me her beautiful smile—the one I never saw until Theo became *her* sunlight. "Damn right you are. Because Morenos kick ass and—"

"—then eat all the cookies for good measure," I finish.

We both grin at each other dopily, the memory of coming up with our Moreno motto a warm blanket to my soul. Then her face grows serious.

"What?" I ask.

She glances over her shoulder at the men on the porch then back to me, concern edging into her expression. "Good thing you're not afraid of hard work."

Clearly, she's seen Theo's distancing over the last couple of hours as much as I have.

"No," I say. "I'm not."

She shakes her head then looks back at me. "Stubborn men."

Seriously.

She squeezes my hand again. "You're a Moreno. You can out-stubborn anyone."

That's the hope, anyway.

"Give him hell, honey," she murmurs. "Don't let him shut you out."

I narrow my eyes at the menfolk. "Yeah, no. That shit's stopping here and now."

"Damn right it is." She holds her fist up for me to bump. "Sissy?" she asks after I've done so.

"Yeah?"

"I am so fucking proud of you." Her hand comes to the side of my throat when my mouth drops open. "Not just for working hard and kicking ass, but for knowing that something needs to change. That's scary as fuck and you're amazing for going there."

"Eva—"

"And we *were* in survival mode, for too damned long. I'm just glad that you've seen there's another way."

My whole body has gone still and my eyes are stinging but I manage to hold it together long enough to whisper, "I am so fucking proud of you too."

"I know." She gives me a watery smile. "I love you."

"I love you too."

She sniffs.

I sniff.

God, this is why Morenos don't do sappy.

It's hell on the mascara...or would be if I was wearing any.

"All right," I say, dashing the back of my hand beneath each eye. "Enough of this. Get your man home"—I jut my chin toward Walker and Theo who are still standing on the porch, albeit now seemingly having an intense discussion—"and leave me to manage mine."

She exhales, shakes off the seriousness of our bonding moment and grins at me. "That's the spirit." And before I can respond, she shouts, "Squishy!"—which elicits a groan from Theo—"Let's go!"

To his credit—after the groan—Theo just thumps Walker on the back and bounds down the steps, stopping only to sweep me into a hug. "It was good to see you tonight, sweetheart."

"You too, Theo."

He tugs at a lock of my hair. "Don't be a stranger at our place either, yeah?"

I nod.

"And don't worry"—he winks—"I won't let your sister storm the defenses all too often."

I laugh, but I barely get it out before a growl hits my ears and I'm tugged away from Theo, held tightly against Walker's big, strong chest.

Theo smirks, but doesn't protest, just calls out his goodbye as he gets into the car.

My gaze catches Eva's, and I see that she's smirking too.

But I don't get a chance to do more than glare at her before that big, strong chest behind me rumbles in anger.

"Are you fucking serious?" Walker growls, the question hot in my ear.

I turn...

And find myself staring up into furious brown eyes.

Thirty-Five

"What's the matter?" she asks.

"It's cold," I snap, wrapping the jacket I grabbed from the hook inside around her shoulders.

Grabbed because this fucking woman has been standing out in the cold in nothing but a T-shirt, jeans, and socks for the better part of twenty minutes as she talked with her sister.

Without a coat.

Or fucking *shoes.*

I glare down and her and start herding her toward the house, ignoring Theo smirking at me through his windshield and Eva's gleeful expression, and when Dommie doesn't move fast enough, I decide—*fuck it*—and scoop her up, cradling her against my chest as I carry her up the walk.

"What are you doing?" she snaps, pushing at my chest.

"Hush," I mutter, taking us up the two steps that lead onto the porch, reaching for the handle and moving us through the door. Taking us inside.

Where I can get this woman warm.

"Did you just tell me to *hush?*" she asks, tone deadly.

I shut the wooden panel behind us, flick the lock, then look down into her eyes, holding them, seeing the murder in their depths—murder that grows—as I say, "Yes."

Her nails dig sharply into my chest. "Put me down. Right *now.*"

"No," I mutter, bypassing the living room and kitchen, keeping her close as I move to the stairs, take them up to the second floor, to my bedroom.

I dump her on the bed.

She gasps, starts to sit up, but I place my hand in the middle of her chest, press her down then bend so I can tug her socks from her feet, tossing the cold, wet material to the side.

Her skin is like ice so I cup them in my palms, rubbing them briskly.

"You did," she said. "You actually told me to *hush.*"

I ignore her, move to the other foot, warming it.

"I can't believe—"

"Dommie," I grit out. "Please just be quiet."

A beat of silence. Then she seems to study me closely—*seems* because I'm focused on her foot, on the pale blue polish on her nails, her delicate toes, the slender arch along the bottom, the single freckle she has on top.

I close my eyes, bend and press my lips to the freckle.

"Walker," she whispers.

I settle her foot onto the mattress, tug the blankets over her.

Her expression is...

Damn.

She sees too much.

And I know...I can't do this.

"I can't *fucking* do this."

Her hand settles on top of mine, startling me, making me realize that the words I thought were just in my head had been spoken aloud, that *I* had spoken out loud.

"You can't do what?" she asks softly.

"This," I blurt. "*Us.*"

I straighten, start to push off the bed, but then her fingers have wrapped around my wrist in a surprisingly strong grip, halting me when I would have run. "I need to go," I practically beg—yes, *beg.* But it's like I can't stop myself, like I'm standing outside of my body as panic has my mind shutting down.

If she finds out, she'll look at me differently.

If she finds out, she'll leave me.

If she finds out...she'll hate me.

"I'm going to quit," she whispers.

I still. "What?"

"I'm going to shut down Dommie's Cakes—no new orders, no opening the stall at the arena, no guilting myself into working until I feel like I can't breathe..."

My heart starts pounding.

She presses her lips flat, releases them. "The lease for my apartment is up in a month and Eva says I can move in with them so I can go to school and figure what I want to do and just...breathe for a few months until I know what I want."

"*No.*" The word is torn from me, ripped from my throat.

Hurt starts creeping into her face. "I would think that you, of everyone around me, would think I'm making the right choice in making these changes."

"No," I say again. "I mean, yes, I'm proud of you, baby. Proud that you're taking the time to figure out what you want."

Her brows pull together.

"I—just... Don't move in with Eva and Theo. Stay with me. Move in *here.*"

She shakes her head and my stomach sinks.

"Baby," I begin.

She squeezes my wrist. "You can't even talk to me about what's going on in your head, what you're clearly too scared to share with me. You shut me down earlier and barely looked at me these last hours, and"—a breath—"you still haven't told me why you broke up with me months ago."

My stomach convulses.

"You know everything in my head," she murmurs. "You said you love—"

I stiffen.

Because I do.

But, fuck, what if she thinks...

Her eyes close for a moment then open, and the determination in them makes me feel like even more of a coward. "You know what's in my head and heart and haven't judged me, haven't looked at me differently—even though they are some of my biggest fears and insecurities and shameful secrets."

"Because they're nothing like what—" I break off, grind my teeth together.

"Like what's inside you?" she asks.

Bile burns the back of my throat.

"I'm not like you," I say, tugging at my arm, but not very hard. Because of the conflict inside me. Because maybe part of me knows that if I lose the tether of her hold, I'll lose her forever. "I'm not strong—not anywhere but the ice, anyway. My parents are fuckups, but I'm even more of one. I knew exactly what it was like to be the kid between them and—"

Her fingers tighten enough that I realize what I'm saying.

Realize how close I've slipped to the edge.

And the words stopper up.

"Do you—" Her throat works. "Do you have a kid?"

"No," I rasp.

Her body is still, so fucking still for a second, then she shakes her head. "Honey..."

I clench my jaw so hard that pain shoots through it, every part of me hating this, hating what I'm holding inside, and...wanting to let it out, to exorcise it, knowing that Dommie is maybe the one person on this planet who won't judge me for it.

But the shame wells up, claws at my throat and the words won't come.

She sees it too, disappointment growing in her eyes, her grip loosening and her hand sliding free.

"So," she says quietly. "You want me to be in a relationship with you, you want to know everything in my heart and mind and soul, you want me to love you, but you don't want to—or *can't* do the same in return."

"I—"

She drops her chin to her chest, exhales. "I'm not going to give you ultimatums and demand you divulge all of your secrets. That's not fair." She lifts her head, stares deeply into my eyes. "I just...considering all the ways I've grown over the last weeks, all the things I've learned about myself and how I've finally started to come to terms with what I want and deserve, I don't think that I can be in a relationship—long term—with someone who can't give me the same openness in return that I'm willing to give."

"Sunlight—"

"That's just it," she murmurs. "You *say* I'm that, but I don't think that's actually the truth."

I freeze.

Her expression is so damned earnest. "I *want* to be that for you—the person who can guide you through, the person you turn to. I want to help you like you've helped me. That's what you do when you love someone."

I choke.

"Yes," she murmurs, pushing off the bed and moving toward me. She drops her hand to my chest, resting it over my heart. "I love you, Walker. I've loved you for a long time, even though I couldn't see past myself to understand what I was feeling. And"— she drops her hand, sending ice skating through my veins—"I love you enough to demand that we do better for each other."

Thirty-Six

Dommie

Walking out of the bedroom and shoving my feet into my shoes—without socks since the man I love was so damned worried about warming me up, he'd taken them off, caressed my cold skin—is one of the hardest things I've ever done.

Harder even than thinking through what I want with the bakery, with my career, with my future.

I want Walker.

But I also want what my sister has, what Kailey and Smitty have.

I want the man who loves me to not hold anything back.

It's not enough to be coddled and taken care of. It's not enough for him to be thoughtful and kind. Maybe that makes me an asshole who is demanding too much.

But I finally understand that I need something different, something more.

I *need* to be able to be an equal partner.

Exhaling, I start moving down the stairs, heading for the

garage, but just before I'm about to snag my purse off the kitchen counter, the doorbell rings.

"Dammit," I mutter, thinking that someone must have forgotten something—or maybe that Eva decided to come back for more pizza (and gossip)—and rotate around, start walking toward the door. My hand lands on the knob and I'm turning it—

"Dommie!"

My heart leaps and I jerk, gaze going over my shoulder, seeing Walker pounding down the stairs.

Coming after me.

Thank God.

"Wait," he says. "I need—"

I don't realize that my hand's still on the knob.

Not until the door is shoved in, slamming into my side, my head, jamming my arm back, wrenching my wrist. I gasp in pain, jerking my hand free, spinning back to catch the now-open door, and face the person on the other side.

It's not Eva.

Or Smitty trying to circle back for gossip.

It's...

I don't know.

A slender blonde with a little boy at my side.

A slender blonde I've seen before.

Months ago. Right after Walker pushed me away.

Do you have a kid?

No.

So why does that little boy have the same color eyes?

A soft curse, but then Walker is at my back, tugging me away from the door, gently sliding a hand down my aching side. "You okay?"

I nod.

"Mom?" I hear, drawing my focus from Walker, returning it to the two people standing just outside the front door.

"Who's this?" the woman snaps, eyes shooting laser beams at

me. "And why the fuck has she been staying at your house? Why is she hosting fucking *parties in your house?!*" The question ends on a shriek and I inch closer to Walker, wanting away from the woman,

"You shouldn't be here," Walker growls, tucking me behind him. "And you know it."

I look away from Laser Eyes, turn my gaze to Walker. He's focused on the woman, his jaw so tight I can see a muscle flexing beneath his skin, and his grip on me...is *firm*—actually it's bordering on the *wrong* side of firm.

"*Mom*," I hear again, more urgently.

The woman takes a step toward us.

"*Don't*," Walker snaps, thrusting his hand out. "Or I'm calling Detective McKay again."

"Mom!" A tug at her sleeve. "I have to go to the bathroom."

I suck in a breath, feel Walker do the same.

"Not now," the woman snaps. "Walker—"

"Don't say another word," Walker growls before shifting his gaze to the boy with those eerily similar brown eyes. His big shoulders rise and fall on a breath. His tone gentles. "You remember where it is from last time?"

The boy's *little* shoulders relax and he nods, says quietly. "Yeah."

"Good," Walker murmurs. "Go ahead. We'll wait here."

He shifts, nudging me further behind him and moving us to the side so that the boy can slip through.

The kiddo slides by us, and I watch as he disappears into the half-bath just off the hallway.

"No," Walker says, his body tensing.

Then rocking backward.

As though...someone pushed him.

What the actual fuck?

I look around his body, see that his arm is up again, his palm held straight out. Something the blonde ignores as shoves forward and runs into it, stumbling back, barely able to keep from falling.

"You asshole," the woman screams coming forward again. "You fucking cheating, lying asshole!"

His body rocks again. She stumbles back a second time.

Fucking hell.

"Do you have your phone?" he asks me quietly, ignoring the shoving and the shouting.

"Yes," I say, starting to dig into my purse.

"You fucking prick! Don't you dare call the police! Don't you —" She sucks in a breath, the vitriol stopping for a brief respite and I hear the toilet flush behind us, the sink turn on, which is a surprise, frankly, considering the boy can't be more than seven or eight.

A good kid.

My heart squeezes, and she starts yelling again, drowning out the sounds behind me as I get my phone out.

Another breath and the bathroom door opens with a quiet squeak.

Footsteps on the floor.

"Dial this number," Walker says, tone neutral, but a little louder when she starts up again, and I punch in the digits on my screen, hit the call button then pass it up to him.

He puts it to his ear.

"John," he says after a moment. "She's back." A pause. "Yeah," he mutters, "I bet you can hear her too." A beat. "Yeah, thanks." He pulls the phone from his ear, passes it back to me.

I tuck it away and—

"Excuse me."

The boy's soft voice reaches my ears, and my heart squeezes.

But Walker doesn't seem affected as he just shifts to the side, allows the kiddo to pass.

"You fucking ass—"

"Right," Walker mutters, herding me back. "We're done here."

"No we're not. We are fucking *not*—"

He rocks back hard enough that I know he was pushed, a-

fucking-gain, but then he's closing the door, closing her out, closing—

He spins to face me. "Are you okay?"

"I—" I shake my head, my eyes going to the scratches raking down his chest, his arm, raised red lines that make me want to kill the bitch on the porch.

Gentle fingers on my temple. "Shit, baby, you're going to have a bruise."

"I—"

Pound. Pound. Pound.

"Walker, open this fucking door right now!"

"He has your eyes," I whisper.

His shoulders slump, and he whispers back. "I know."

Something inside me breaks off, disappears into space. "I—"

But I don't get to finish speaking. Maybe it's a good thing because I don't know what the hell I'm going to say, anyway.

Maybe something like—

You have a son?

Why did you lie to me not ten minutes ago?

Or maybe, more importantly—

How could you leave him with a woman like that?

HOW?

But I don't get any of those questions out because there's the *bloop* of a siren ringing out and the woman's voice increases in volume, in pitch, until she's practically screeching.

No.

Until she *is* screeching.

And then there's a different knock—this one authoritative.

"Stand back," Walker orders quietly.

I take a step away, losing the warmth of him, but gaining the distance I need, considering my head is spinning.

Is this why?

Why he's worked so hard to keep me away from knowing the truth about him?

I don't get answers to those questions.

Because he's opening the door and we're facing two police officers standing on the front porch.

———

"You guys got here fast," Walker says a little while later, standing on the other side of the island. "I knew that you had my back. I just didn't know it was this much."

He's put a shirt on, covering up those scratches marring his bare chest.

The woman is in the back of a squad car.

The kid—last I saw—is sitting on the porch next to one of the officers who initially showed up.

"Neighbors called it in when she started yelling," Detective McKay says—the same man I gave my statement to about Professor Johnson all those weeks ago. "They were already on their way when you called." A slight pause then, "I think it's time, Walk."

Time for what, I don't know.

I *do* know that the statement has Walker's hands tightening into fists, his knuckles standing out in sharp relief.

"John," he says. "I don't want to draw any more attention to—"

"If you don't press charges this is going to keep happening," John says quietly. "And what if you're not here next time." A beat. "And Dommie is."

Walker's head shoots up, his eyes locking onto mine.

They're an empty slate and disappointment bursts through me.

Because he still has that wall up.

Because things aren't ever going to change.

Because...I want more.

And I don't think he's capable of giving it to me.

THIRTY-SEVEN

WALKER

I see it in her face.

She's giving up on me.

But having her walk out of my bedroom, knowing she was prepared to walk out of my life made me see...

Fear.

Anger.

Pride in her strength.

And reason.

I can't let her go.

Even if the shame is heavy and the words struggle to come and she might look at me differently.

Even if...

I lose her anyway.

Because she deserves to know the truth of me—to know *all* of me.

"Ben went into the bathroom," I tell John. "Neither of us has been in there since. Can you—"

I watch Dommie frown, but John has been around long

enough to get it, to have seen it all, to know the lengths that Kaitlyn would go to get back at me.

He nods. "I'll check."

"Check for what?" Dommie asks after he leaves the room.

"Ben isn't my son," I say quietly.

Her head shoots up, eyes locking with mine, and she worries her bottom lip with her teeth.

"I thought—" The words stopper up but I push through. "When she showed up back in October"—I know she tracks the date, starts putting the pieces together, but I keep going—"I thought he was mine," I whisper. "I mean, fuck, he looks like me, and I knew—despite the shit that went down between Kaitlyn and me, I wouldn't miss anymore of his life, wouldn't make him a pawn, like I'd been."

She shifts, moving around the counter and stopping close to me.

"I got a paternity test," I say. "First thing, even though she fought it, even though some part of me knew it couldn't be all that simple because of the way she refused. But my lawyers got it ordered and..."

I watch her shoulders tense. Then they drop slightly, and she reaches out to take my hand. "Tell me," she murmurs.

And...I do.

"Ben isn't mine."

Her fingers squeeze. "Why didn't you say something back then?" she asks quietly. "You had—have—to know I would never fault you for something like that."

"I know," I whisper. "But that's..." Her fingers squeeze again when I falter. "That's not all of it."

"Tell me, honey."

"She—" I take a breath, brace myself, knowing that I need Dommie to understand, knowing that John is going to come back from searching the bathroom at some point, so I have to stop fucking dragging my feet and tear off the goddamned Band-Aid. "Earlier tonight, when we were about to..." I slant a look at her and she nods. "I-I froze because...*fuck*," I mutter, shoving my free hand through my hair. Why is this so fucking hard?

"It's okay," she says. "You don't have to—"

"It's because I've had a woman tell me that before, tell me she was on birth control and we can skip the condom. Because *Kaitlyn* said it before and..." My eyes slide closed. Maybe it's cowardly, but I can't look at her face when she hears the rest. "I didn't want to," I murmur. "I barely knew her and wasn't comfortable, but I was drunk and then she was on top of me and then she was fucking me and, *God*—"

I break off, hating that my voice cracks.

"I told her no," I whisper. "That I didn't want it, and—"

Dommie wraps her arms around me. "It's not your fault, honey."

I shudder.

"And I'm so sorry that she did that to you."

The words won't stop now. "When she showed up saying he was mine, demanding money, I knew if he was my son, I would shove all that down, push past it, give him the life he deserves. Because I wouldn't be like my parents were to me. But I also knew as things went on and Kaitlyn became even more of a fucking nightmare that I couldn't do that to you, couldn't drag you along, especially with her acting crazy and showing up at all hours and—"

"Drugs in the bathroom."

Dommie stiffens, her head shooting up, turning toward Detective McKay who's walking back into the kitchen with an evidence bag held up in front of him.

"What?" she whispers.

I touch her cheek. "It's not his fault," I say. "He's just doing what his mom makes him—"

She squeezes my waist then rotates around to face John. "Drugs?" she asks and her tone has gone icy.

John studies her for a long moment then flicks his eyes up to mine, rightly reading I haven't gotten to that part yet. "I'll be back."

His boots clomp on the floor as he walks out of the kitchen.

A second later, Dommie is facing me again, her stare blazing with fury. "You're telling me the woman who assaulted you today has assaulted you before—assaulted you in the worst fucking way—"

I grasp her shoulders. "Baby."

"—and she has her kid who's what? Eight? Planting drugs for her in *your* bathroom after—af-after—"

I see it all hit her then in the way her voice cracks and her eyes fill with tears and—

"Fuck, honey," she whispers, tears clinging to her lashes. "*This* is why you broke up with me? These are your *reasons?*"

"I couldn't let her into your life," I begin, rubbing the throb at the edge of my forehead. "She's done this before. Showed up, hit me, screamed and made a scene, planted shit to try to black-mail me with. If John, if Detective McKay hadn't helped me, I would be totally fucked, and I couldn't do that to you. I *couldn't—*"

Her hands come to either side of my jaw, turning my face back to hers. "Stop it," she says. "Don't you fucking dare put her bull-shit onto you. She raped you, took something from you that is precious, that she absolutely shouldn't have. And she's continued to violate you ever since. The stalking. The drugs. Assaulting you, and—" She exhales sharply. "She's the monster, the only one in the wrong here."

"*I'm* the one who pushed you away just when we were getting started. *I'm* the one who hurt you."

Her forehead comes to mine. "Stop," she whispers. "Just stop for a second and let me hold you." Then, before I can protest, before I can keep apologizing, her hands drop from my face to my shoulders, and her arms are wrapping tight around my neck, her body pressing close, her lips are at my ear. "I'm am so fucking sorry she did that to you."

"Baby—"

"And it's not your fault."

My heart convulses. "I should have—"

She pulls back, cups my face again. "It's *not* your fault."

I inhale, cover her hands with my own and peel them from my face, pressing a kiss to each palm. "I'm sorry I hurt you."

"Honey," she whispers then pauses, studies my face. Sighs. "I'm not going to get you to change your mind, am I?"

A shake of my head. "I should have done things differently."

So many fucking things.

Half of her mouth curves up. "I love you."

I settle my forehead against hers. "I—"

"I know," she whispers. "But I'm not done talking."

Unbidden, a chuckle rises up in my throat. "Okay, baby, I'll shut up now."

"Damn right you will." The other half of her mouth twitches. "You can tell me you love me later."

I chuckle again. "Okay, Sunlight."

She lifts her head, holds my eyes, expression going serious. "Thank you for telling me."

Guilt slides through me, stealing my amusement. "I was going to tell you before," I say. "I knew I had to and—"

She brushes her lips over mine. "I know," she murmurs. "I *know*," she says again when I open my mouth to explain. "Honey, I heard you coming down the stairs before I opened the door—or she opened it into me, anyway," she adds, rubbing her shoulder.

More guilt lashing through my insides. "Dammit, Sunlight, I'm—"

Another brush of her lips over mine. "*Stop.*"

I clench my teeth together.

"I have one more question."

Worry ties my insides into knots. "I'll tell you anything."

Tender eyes, a soft hand on my cheek. "Are there..." A breath. "Are there any other hidden *reasons?*"

My mouth falls open. "No, baby. God, isn't all *that*"—I nod toward the front of the house—"enough?"

Quiet laughter, her mouth pressing to mine briefly. "That's more than enough."

"Good," I say, gently touching the bruise forming on her temple. "Then let's get you some ice."

"Just one more thing," she murmurs, her arms wrapping around my shoulders, her body coming close to mine again.

"What's that?"

"You can tell me you love me now."

Thirty-Eight

Dommie

I roll over, having to admit that this sleeping in thing is pretty fucking great.

Especially when I get to wake up with my hockey player next to me.

Even *if* it's in my queen bed in my apartment, instead of the expensive and ridiculously huge eastern king at Walker's place.

At...my place.

Well, it'll be mine in a couple of hours.

Today is my last day in my apartment.

This afternoon...well, Walker's house will officially become my house too.

Sighing, I roll over in the circle of his arms, not trying to escape—not this time—both because I like it here, and because I've reduced my pre-bed liquid intake so I don't need to heed nature's calling first thing in the morning.

Now I get cuddle time.

Walker time.

And—

"Mmm," he murmurs, rolling toward me, big hands drawing

me closer, blazing body pinning me to the mattress. I inhale the spicy scent of him, wind my legs around his waist, my arms around his shoulders and just hold on.

Enjoying him.

Enjoying this time.

Enjoying the present and my life and—

His lips find mine, tongue tracing the seam of my mouth.

I open, not caring about morning breath or that we're both half asleep or that my hair's certainly a mess and the tank top I'm wearing has twisted and my boob is falling out the arm hole.

Not cute.

Not put together.

Just me.

And that's enough.

Our tongues tangle and I moan softly as he kisses me, slow and deep and in absolutely no hurry. His hand is tracing up my side, beneath my tank, caressing my hip and stomach, breasts and nipples.

And then I'm moaning louder, arching against him.

My pussy aches, wanting him inside, even as he displays absolutely no urgency to get there.

Instead, he's driving me crazy. Rolling my nipples, lightly squeezing my breasts. Breaking our kiss and then dragging his mouth along my jaw, down my throat, along that exposed flesh of my boob.

"Oh God," I moan, reaching between us, slipping my hand into his underwear and wrapping my fingers around the hard length of his cock.

I want it in my mouth.

I want it inside.

I want—

Suddenly, I'm flipped over onto my hands and knees, the blankets tossed to the side, and his big body is bent over mine.

My underwear is tugged down.

My tank ripped over my head.

"Fucking beautiful," he groans, nipping at my throat and then straightening enough to trace his palm down my spine *oh so slowly*.

Until it hits the curve of my ass.

And then—

Smack!

I gasp as that sting spreads along my skin, heat blooming between my legs, my pussy convulsing around...nothing.

"Honey," I beg, arching my ass up, begging for his mouth, for his fingers, for his cock.

A nip to my cheek. "Impatient."

"I need you," I murmur.

"Mmm." He nips at the other cheek, and I cry out, arching back, something he takes advantage of as he puts a knee between my thighs, separates them, and...dips his fingers into the heat of me.

Wet.

I'm so fucking wet that they slide right in.

"I love this fucking cunt," he growls. "Love how it clamps around me."

"Walker," I whisper, grinding back against him because it feels fucking great.

But it's also...

Not enough.

"Honey," I say, rocking against him, "I want your cock."

"Mmm," he murmurs, but all he does is keep stroking those long, thick fingers inside me.

And...*fuck*...I drop my head back...that's so fucking good.

Maybe I don't want him to stop.

Maybe he can keep going like that forever.

Which, of course, is the moment that he slips his fingers from inside me.

"What—"

"I want you, baby," he says against my skin, teeth nipping, tongue flicking, the words vibrating through me.

"Then take me," I tell him, extending an arm toward my nightstand, intending to snag the box of condoms.

"No, baby," he murmurs, coming over me, kissing down my spine, coaxing me to roll over onto my back. "I want you, like this. Nothing between us."

I freeze. "*Honey*. I—" My heart is full, so fucking full, but also, I can't help but think this is too soon, that he needs more time. "I'm not sure this is the right time. You just—"

His face—

God, he's giving me...

Gentle.

He's giving me...

Everything.

"I'm ready, baby," he murmurs. "So *fucking* ready." A kiss to my temple, the bruise long faded over the last few weeks. "But only if you are too."

My heart is pounding because this is...a big freaking step.

This is trust.

This is moving forward with no secrets between us.

This is *love*.

I reach up, touch his jaw, and—

"God, I love you," I tell him. "But, I swear to God, if you don't get inside me right now, I'm going to pounce, honey, and use you like my own personal sex toy."

His smile nearly sets me aflame.

"Another time," he says, hand gripping my thigh, pushing my leg wide.

And then the thick head of his cock is notching at my entrance, and he's pushing inside.

There's the stretch, the burn, the filling me to beautiful completion.

I moan, dropping my head back against the pillow, hips rocking so I can take him deeper. His groan rumbles through his chest as he drops a hand by my head, torso pressing to mine, lips brushing along my throat, my jaw, before sealing over my mouth.

His cock is hard and his thrusts are slow and steady and *deep*.

So deep that I'm close in seconds.

That I'm sailing over the edge in not much longer than that.

"Fuck, baby," he groans as I come around him. "Your pussy is gripping me so fucking good."

"I—"

But I don't get a chance to finish that thought—whatever it might be—because he's reaching between us, thumb arrowing straight for my clit, strokes not changing, not stopping, not altering that slow and deep and steady.

It's just that the added friction on that bundle of nerves is fucking *chef's kiss*.

Almost too much and yet not enough.

But, as usual, he reads it, reads *me*, knows exactly what I need.

Those thrusts get harder, and he picks up the speed—and suddenly slow and steady and deep becomes hard and faster and even deeper.

"Oh God," I gasp as I approach the edge again. "Oh my fucking *God.*"

He's close—I can tell in the way his eyes bore into mine, in the gleam of sweat on his forehead, in the rapid breaths tearing through his lungs, the way his strokes aren't exactly steady.

But he's not going down, not without me by his side.

And I'm perfectly fine with that.

Because his cock is hard and big and deep.

Because his thumb is working me.

Because his mouth is coming down on mine again.

That's all I need—or maybe it's that I finally have *everything* I need. His body close, his lips on mine, his cock inside me. Love in the way he fucks me, in his hold, in his kiss, in this moment. And trust—so much fucking trust in me.

I have him—*all* of him, no secrets or *reasons* or distance between us.

And *that's* what sends me over the edge.

"*Walker!*" I cry as I explode.

Sparks behind my eyes, my orgasm blazing through me, tightening every muscle in my body for one long moment, and all of that tense is followed by bliss, by wave after wave of pleasure.

"Fuck, baby," he groans, strokes going wild, losing rhythm as he explodes inside me. "Fucking hell, Sunlight. God that's so fucking—*good.*"

His big body collapses, pressing me into the mattress, stealing all the air from my lungs.

But only for a second before he rolls us to the side, holding me close, bodies intertwined, breaths coming rapidly.

"Good fucking morning," I whisper once I can speak.

Silence.

And then he bursts out laughing.

And I find that's the best sound in the entire world.

THIRTY-NINE

WALKER

I just had the best morning of my fucking life—

Literally my *fucking* life.

And I'm in bed with the woman I love, our future in front of us, no more secrets weighing me down. No more reasons that I'm hiding behind.

Because the shame is gone and I can just be here with her.

She sighs and burrows closer, her nose pressing to the base of my throat.

"I love you," she whispers.

"I'll never get tired of hearing that," I say, smoothing my hand over her hair.

She laughs quietly. "I know the feeling."

Grinning, I roll her to her back, coming over her, staring down into her beautiful eyes. "I love—"

Knock. Knock. Knock!

I freeze, head jerking up, eyes going to the open door of the bedroom, to the darkened hallway, wondering why in the fuck there is always someone knocking on our *goddamned* doors.

Ding dong. Ding dong. Ding dong!

I groan and drop my forehead to hers. "Why does the universe hate me?"

She giggles, fingers skating along my jaw. "You know it's probably the Breakers crew coming to help me move."

I scowl, but because she's probably right, I push off her, losing the tight heat of that gorgeous pussy, the soft curves of her body. "Do what you need to do in the bathroom, baby. I'll make sure the *crew* doesn't bombard the bedroom."

A brush of her lips over mine. "Thanks, honey."

Knock. Knock. KNOCK!

"Jesus Christ," I mutter, climbing out of bed, helping Dommie do the same before I grab my sweats from the floor, step into them, and head for the hall, pausing to watch her sweet ass bounce a little as she strides into the bathroom.

Fucking gorgeous.

Fucking *mine.*

Ding dong. Ding dong. Ding dong!

"All right. All fucking right." I stomp down the hall, wrench open the door, and—

Drop my head back, direct my words up toward the ceiling.

"Are you fucking *kidding* me?"

Professor Johnson. Professor fucking Johnson is standing on Dommie's front porch.

What the *actual* fuck?

"Tell me you're not here," I snap, glancing back down at him, at *Todd*. "Tell me you're *not* fucking here."

He narrows his eyes. "I need to talk to Dommie."

"And *I* want to win the Stanley Cup every fucking season, but miracles don't happen in real life, so fuck off before I call the cops and we press charges for you violating the restraining order."

The professor's eyes narrow. "She didn't call me like she was supposed to. I left my number and—"

I freeze.

The note from Dommie's car.

That fucking bastard.

Todd puffs up his chest, takes a step forward. "—she *didn't* call me."

I brace, fist clenching at my side, wanting to kill this fucker, but not going to throw the first punch.

I will, however, throw the last.

Only, I don't get the chance too.

"Walker, why don't you let them—" Footsteps skid to a halt behind me as Dommie comes close. "Um, honey, that's not Professor Johnson on my front porch, is it?"

"It's *Todd!*" he snaps. "And I'm not here to bother you."

I lift my brows in surprise.

Dommie snorts as she comes to my side. "Well," she mutters. "Mission *not* accomplished."

Todd slices a hand through the air. "I need you to call the university and—"

"Tell them that you're harassing me again?" she asks. "Because if I do that, it's going to be preceded by a call to Detective McKay telling him that you're violating the restraining order I filed, and I don't know if you know this, but the good detective and I are on a first name basis, so I know that he'll haul ass over here."

For the first time, Professor Johnson falters. "You wouldn't."

Dommie lifts her chin. "Just try me."

"I—"

She slips her arm through mine, her body pressing close. "I —" she begins before cutting herself off with a shake of her head. "You know what?" she asks, glancing up at me.

"What?" I say, lifting a hand, extending it, shoving at his chest when he takes a step toward her.

"I think we can—"

Todd stumbles backward, turns, and please—fucking *please*— let him walking away be him walking the fuck out of our lives.

"—just...close the door and practice our ignoring skills."

Which is precisely what she does, gripping the edge of the wooden panel and swinging it shut.

Knock. Knock. Knock!

Todd, apparently, has not decided to walk out of our lives.

Not yet, anyway.

She takes my hand, pulls me toward the hall. "We're investing in a camera equipped doorbells."

"You already have one," I point out.

"Okay fine," she says, mouth tipping up. "We're investing in speedy internet so they always work and then actually checking them before we answer the door."

I grin. "Fair enough."

Ding dong. Ding dong. Ding dong!

"And we're keeping Detective McKay on speed dial."

"Also fair enough."

She grins, makes the call, and we continue practicing our ignoring skills by retreating to the bedroom and practicing some *other* skills. "Maybe we should move somewhere that's behind a gate," she says a while later.

I stroke a finger along her jaw. "With a guard tower? And barbed wire?" I tease, thinking about the fact that *I've* filed a restraining order of my own, along with assault charges, but that last thing I heard from my lawyer—and the private investigator she hired—was that Kaitlyn had moved back to California and was living with a professional soccer player.

Heaven help him.

I just hope that means she's moved on from thinking I'm going to give her anything other than rides in the back of police cars.

"Barbed wire might be taking it a little far."

I kiss her cheek. "Well, just keep it in the suggestion box, yeah?"

She laughs, opens her mouth—

Knock. Knock. Knock!

We both groan.

But this time, she utilizes her phone.

And the app for the camera doorbell.

And we see...

The Breakers Crew has arrived to help with the move.

Which might be the first pleasant surprise on the other side of a door we've had in…

Well, maybe ever.

So, I'm taking it.

And the moving help.

EPILOGUE

DOMMIE, FIVE YEARS LATER

"Why did I know I would find you here?" Walker says quietly, and I freeze, lifting the tip of the piping bag away from the cake.

I know my expression is guilty, but I don't cop to it.

Instead, I set the bag to the side, move across the room, and hug my hockey player tight.

He's got dark circles under his eyes, and I know this is the point of the season where fatigue is setting in and road games are tough and he's exhausted after a late flight home.

But...

It's our son's third birthday tomorrow.

"Wyatt's cake needs to be perfect," I say, moving toward him, pressing close, doing my favorite thing ever when he comes home from a road trip—just hugging him.

"Of course it will be," he says, arms wrapping around me in turn, one hand landing on the center of my back and rubbing gently, the other settling on my nape, under my hair, massaging the tight muscles there. "Because you're making it."

I smile and inhale the spicy scent of him, feeling the rightness settling over me.

"How did the opening go?" he asks after a couple of moments, releasing me to place his palm on the slightly rounded curve of my belly. "And how's my little girl doing?"

"She's perfect," I murmur. "Just like the opening. The cases were sold out in just a couple of hours."

The *bakery* cases.

Because I found my niche—and it doesn't involve waking up at ungodly hours and working six days a week, decorating cakes until my hands barely work, taking orders until I can't breathe because I'm so worried about supporting myself that I'm too scared to turn down a single one.

Instead, I've put my MBA to good use managing Ren's bakeries.

Yup.

Bakeries. *Plural.*

I love making the spreadsheets and business plans. I love the hiring and scheduling. I love balancing books and filing taxes and putting in supply orders. And, most especially, I love that I've found my enjoyment in baking and decorating again.

When I want to.

For the people I love.

And without any of that clawing, desperate need to keep working so I can survive.

So I can avoid living.

Nope.

My life is full—and about to get fuller—and...

I have a cake to decorate.

A party to prep for.

"Want to get ready for bed, honey?" I murmur. "I'll finish the cake and join you."

"Yes, you *will* join me," he says, scooping me up and bringing me well away from the cake—*and* my piping bag. "Because you can finish the cake later—"

"But—"

He starts walking, carrying me out of the kitchen.

And…I know that I'm not going to win this battle. Or maybe I don't want to win it.

Because I know where he's taking me.

I know where I want to be.

I know—

Knock. Knock. Knock.

Both of us freeze and glance at the clock above the stove, noting the ungodly hour, and then we look back at each other.

"Phone, Sunlight," he murmurs.

I pull it out of the pocket of my pajamas, open up the camera app, and we both suck in a breath.

"Are you fucking kidding me?"

Because it's not a manipulative woman on the porch who's found her bank account of a man and hasn't bothered us since.

Nor is it a professor who doesn't know the meaning of a boundary.

And it's not a group of nosy hockey players, barging their way in for free pizza or baked goods.

It's…

"A freaking raccoon," I whisper, my lips curving up.

"I told you not to give them marshmallows," he murmurs back.

Which is true.

It was just when they came to the back door a couple of weeks ago with those little hands and sniffing noses and pleading eyes…

I grabbed the first thing close at hand and tossed out some marshmallows.

"Should we?" I nod toward the pantry, toward my stash of mini marshmallows.

"No fucking way," he says, striding into the hall, heading for the stairs. "As someone very smart and very beautiful"—he strokes a finger down the side of my cheek—"once told me. We can just close—or in this case, *leave* it closed—the door and practice our ignoring skills."

"But they're hungry," I whisper.

A flash of wicked in his smile. *"I'm* hungry."

Heat in my belly, liquid between my thighs. "Well," I tease, pushing lightly at his chest. "We can't have that. I'll make you something to...*eat!*"

I squeal as he pretends to drop me then moan when his lips come to mine, tongue slipping into my mouth, hands getting to work.

Because we've reached our bedroom.

Because he's settled me on the mattress, and his big body has come down over mine.

Because his hands have gotten to work—and he's always known what I like, always known how to play my body, how to bring me pleasure. And his years of study in it since we've been together have fine-tuned his skills.

"So fucking beautiful," he groans, lips dragging along my skin.

Down. Down. *Down.*

I part my legs before he gets there, head falling back when he does, moans tumbling off my lips—

Knock-knock. Knock-knock. Knock!

Not from the front door—or the back, for that matter.

And not from an adult hand.

And—instantly—pleasure is no longer on my mind.

Walker groans softly, lips curving as he lifts his head, his eyes meeting mine.

"Mama!" Wyatt cries, his little voice ringing through the door.

"I've got him," my husband says, tugging the blankets up and over me then moving quickly to the door. He opens it and slips out, his soft, "Hey, bub. Why are you awake?" barely reaching my ears.

I grunt as I struggle to sit up and move the blankets to the side.

Wyatt needs me.

But even before I make it upright, I hear, "Daddy!"

"Hi, bub," Walker murmurs. "I missed you."

"I missed you too," my son says in his little voice, rolling the m and y. Then he rules out any chance of a quick bedtime when he asks, still in that sweet, little voice, "Hot cocoa?"

There's a pause.

But I already know what Walker's answer is going to be.

"Yeah, bud. We can have hot cocoa."

There's a squeal of excitement that signifies Wyatt going back to bed is long, long away.

Walker pops his head in, chagrined smile on his face. "Hot cocoa?"

"I definitely want hot cocoa," I say, lifting my arms, silently asking for help in getting this pregnant body upright. His face gentles and then he and Wyatt are moving toward me, each taking a hand and pulling me the rest of the way up.

We go downstairs and I finish decorating the cake while Walker makes us hot chocolate.

Bedtime doesn't happen for a good long while.

But that's okay.

Because we're living a big, beautiful life that blazes bright.

And because...we can sleep in.

———

JACKSON

"So, yeah, he hurt me," Claire says, her voice laced with pain. "Just not how you think."

The locker room goes quiet, awkward, and I feel like a dick, having asked Claire the question in the first place.

I just...

It never fucking crossed my mind to think that someone

would stand her up—or that, worse, someone would get a look at her and not want to worship at her fucking feet.

Beautiful, sweet, quiet, but with a spine of steel Claire deserves the world.

And that fucker who was supposed to take her on a date had hurt her.

So...I'm going to kill the bastard.

She spins on her heel before I can get his full name, address, and social security number, and hurries from the room.

And...I don't think.

I just follow her, trailing her until we're out of earshot, letting her put some space between us and the locker room. But I catch her arm when she turns the corner and would've stepped into a hall with a floor that isn't covered with skate mats.

A hall that has a floor where I can't follow her.

"Claire," I say, drawing her back against me.

"Don't," she whispers.

I spin her so she's facing me, cup her cheek in one palm, willing her to understand how fucking precious she is. "He's an asshole and you deserve better."

Her eyes flick to mine, and then away. "Sure."

Rage in my belly, burning up the back of my throat. How does this woman not see how fucking perfect she is?

"Claire," I begin.

"I'm fine," she whispers, trying to pull free.

But I'm done with this, done with keeping my distance. I draw her with me as I turn and move us through a door and into one of the empty rooms lining the hallway, closing it behind us, pinning her back against the wooden panel.

She's tall for a woman, but I'm taller, especially in my skates. "You're not fine."

Her chin lifts. "I *am* fine."

"Liar."

She shoves at my chest and when that doesn't move me, she

tosses her hands up. "It wasn't going to work long-term anyway, I knew that going in."

"Why wouldn't it work?"

She frowns at me. "Um...because I live in Baltimore and can't have a states away boyfriend?"

Snark.

Sass.

This woman only gives them to me.

And I fucking *love* it.

"So, why did you go on the date in the first place?" My hands are on either side of her head and I sneak them in a little, allowing my fingertips to brush the silken ends of her ponytail.

So fucking soft.

Like I know the rest of her will be.

Her cheeks go pink. "It doesn't matter."

And *that* reaction tells me that it matters a whole fucking lot. "Claire," I warn.

She scowls at me. "Don't pull that big, broody hockey player nonsense. You can't bully me into giving you an answer and—"

"—you don't owe me any explanation of your life," I finish, am able *to* finish because she's told me the same thing enough times that I've memorized her answer.

Those eyes narrow further. "Exactly."

"So," I say, ignoring the laser beams she's tossing my direction and pushing for an answer anyway. "Did you just need to get laid?"

Pink turns to bright red and she shoves harder at my chest. "You're an asshole, you know that, right?"

"Yup."

A huffed-out breath. "Back up," she snaps. "I have work to do."

"Been a long time, kitty cat?" I ask, leaning more heavily against her, wishing I wasn't mostly dressed in my gear, wishing I could feel her naked skin against my own.

"I—*no*."

But there's something in her tone, in the way panic enters her eyes that has me freezing, leaning even closer, studying her face.

"Why then?"

Her jaw clenches and I know she's not going to tell me—know that I can push and push, but that she'll double down and won't *fucking* tell me.

I inhale the sweet scent of her, commit the notes of it to memory.

And then I avoid pushing and commence with...pissing her off.

"So," I say dryly, "you're getting enough dick at home that you don't need sex. What then?" I tap a finger to my chin, watching as her frown deepens. "You just want a guy to buy you dinner and drinks?"

She sputters. "That's n-not—"

"Ah, I see. Don't worry. I'm sure I can talk to someone and put in a good word for you," I cajole. "See about getting you a raise. Or maybe I'll talk to the guys and do a collection, get you some gift cards for Red Lobster or something."

Her eyes say she's going to kill me.

But the devil in me can't stop.

"Not Red Lobster?" I say. "Fine. You drive a hard bargain, but I'm sure I can swing a meal at The Cheesecake Factory—"

"Fuck. You," she hisses.

I shrug and then push a button I know will get her talking. "It's not me who's trying to get laid while on the road."

"I told you—" she growls and shoves at my chest. "I didn't want sex *or* a free meal. I just wanted to go on a real date—" She clamps her lips together, cheeks flaring, eyes darting away, chin dropping.

Fuck.

A *real* date?

"Sweetheart," I rumble.

Her head flies up. "Don't," she snaps, jabbing a finger into my chest. "Don't pretend to care about me."

"That's not fair, I—"

I want to say I *do* care, but that would involve admitting shit that I can't and...

Fuck.

But the shitstorm in my mind doesn't matter.

Because she's rolling her eyes and saying, "Okay fine. You want to know my sad sob story? Really? You do, right? You want to know the whole pathetic truth? I've *never* been laid, okay?"

Every muscle in my body tightens.

"I've never even been on a real date. Hell, I'm so pathetic"—she tosses up her hands again—"that I've never even been kissed!"

She's fucking beautiful.

And furious and smart and sweet and untouched, apparently, and—

Mine.

The most important thing is that she's *mine.*

I cup her jaw, tilt her face up. "Well, I can at least solve *that* one for you."

Her brows draw together. "What—?"

No more words.

We've exchanged *enough* fucking words these last couple of seasons.

It's time for action.

So, I bend...

And press my mouth to hers.

———

Thank you for reading! I hope you loved Dommie and Walker's journey to their HEA as much as I did writing it! The next book in the Breakers Hockey series is BOUND. **She's innocent...and I'm the one who's going to corrupt her.**

CLICK HERE TO READ BOUND NOW>

———

Are you ready to meet Lake Jordan, star forward for the Sierra, wedding officiant extraordinaire, and the man everyone hates to play against, and the woman who steals her way into his grumpy, broody heart? Lake and Nova's book, OVER THE LINE, is available now!

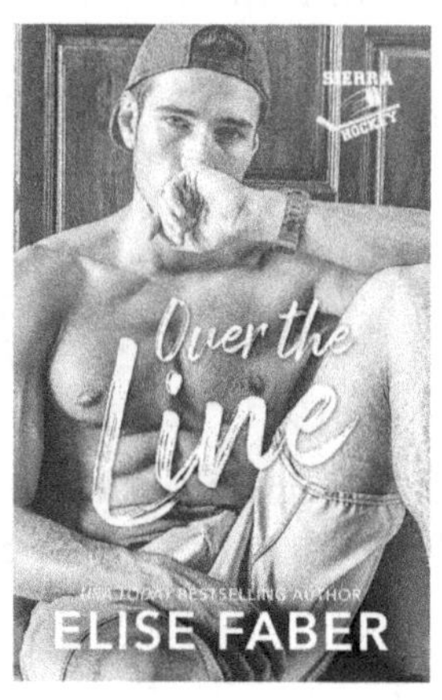

CLICK HERE TO GET OVER THE LINE NOW>

———

And don't miss my brand new hockey romance, BROKEN LACES. **I'm in love with the owner's daughter. But I can't have her...because if I do I'll lose everything.**
CLICK HERE TO READ BROKEN LACES NOW>

If you enjoy my series, considering supporting me on PATREON! Get access to early releases, bonus content, character art, audiobooks, special edition covers, swag, and much more!

CLICK HERE TO SUPPORT ME>